AIRPORTS, EXES, AND OTHER THINGS I'M OVER

AIRPORTS, EXES, AND OTHER THINGS I'M OVER

Shani Petroff

Swoon READS
NEW YORK

A Swoon Reads Book

An imprint of Feiwel and Friends and Macmillan Publishing Group, LLC
175 Fifth Avenue, New York, NY 10010

AIRPORTS, EXES, AND OTHER THINGS I'M OVER. Copyright © 2018 by Shani Petroff. All rights
reserved. Printed in the United States of America.

Our books may be purchased in bulk for promotional, educational, or business use. Please
contact your local bookseller or the Macmillan Corporate and Premium Sales Department at
(800) 221-7945 ext. 5442 or by e-mail at MacmillanSpecialMarkets@macmillan.com.

Library of Congress Cataloging-in-Publication Data is available.
ISBN 978-1-250-13050-1 (hardcover) / ISBN 978-1-250-13052-5 (ebook)

Book design by Carol Ly

First edition, 2018

10 9 8 7 6 5 4 3 2 1

swoonreads.com

FOR MY BROTHER AND COUSINS—AN INCREDIBLE CREW THAT
I WAS LUCKY ENOUGH TO GROW UP ALONGSIDE. HAVING YOU
(AND YOUR FABULOUS SIGNIFICANT OTHERS & KIDS) IN MY LIFE
IS SOMETHING FOR WHICH I WILL ALWAYS BE GRATEFUL.

ONE

Could people actually pass out from excitement? I was starting to think so as I clutched my best friend Trina Gibson's arm. My body was trembling. Literally. I didn't even know that could happen. Sure, in rom-coms and steamy, smutty novels, but in real life? Come on. Yet, here I was shaking like a kindergartener desperately in need of a bathroom. All because Kevin Wayward, music god, had taken the stage, and *I*, Sari Silver, music god wannabe, was there to witness it firsthand. There wasn't even an adjective to explain what I was feeling. Exhilarated, elated, ecstatic, euphoric, some other e-word? All I knew was that this was where I needed to be.

It didn't matter that I didn't get a table, despite getting to the club a couple of hours early and being subjected to two less-than-stellar (to put it nicely) bands, or that I was squished next to my best friend and a bunch of strangers up against a musty-smelling wall. The discomfort was worth it. Spring break was beginning in the most kick-ass way possible.

"We are actually here. This is really happening," I said, practically squealing.

"I know," Trina said. "We earned this." She held up her free arm, the one I wasn't latched onto, and the fluorescent green wristband slid down her dark-brown skin.

"Yes, we did." Everyone in the music world knew the Meta Club. Countless legends got their start there, and often returned to perform. Trina and I wanted in. It was a twenty-one and over club, but we didn't let that stop us. There were months of failed fake ID attempts, begging, singing outside the club until we sweet-talked (or bugged to death, depending on who you talked to) them into letting us in. Since then we'd seen so many amazing shows, and tonight was the icing on the cake. Sure, we had to wear wristbands that kept the bartenders from serving us drinks, but who cared? We were in Meta, and the place gave me a natural buzz.

Kevin held up his hands to quiet the crowd, and I grabbed Trina tighter. I was about to hear Kevin Wayward live. There was a good chance I really was going to lose consciousness.

"As some of you know," he said. "I wandered into this little club in the Village five years ago and, well, the rest is history." History that included getting discovered his first time performing here and going on to win five Grammys—something I would kill for. "But I haven't forgotten my start and that's why I'm back tonight."

Everyone started screaming and applauding again, and Trina turned to me. "That's going to be you someday."

I crossed my fingers *and* my toes. "Hopefully."

"Definitely," she said.

I knew she was just being a good best friend, but I couldn't help praying her words would come true. The image of people lining up to see Sari Silver in concert washed over me. It was what I wanted more than anything.

Kevin Wayward picked up his guitar, stepped closer to the mic, and within seconds let his music pour out. Chills ran through my body. He was so good. It wasn't just that his voice was raw and soulful but that his lyrics were haunting and catchy at the same time. It was just him and his guitar, but it was enough. If I could affect people with my music even a portion of the way he did, I'd be very happy.

By the time Kevin finished his set, I'll admit, I was in total awe. In one song the guy had me almost in tears, the next totally wanting to kiss my boyfriend, and the last tapping my foot and singing along with the rest of the audience at the top of my lungs. Listening to his recordings was nothing compared to hearing him live—it was like the emotions registered ten times higher.

My hands were numb from clapping so hard. "That was incredible," I said, once the room died down. Trina and I moved to a nearby table. Another act was about to take the stage, but the room had pretty much cleared out once Kevin left. "I cannot believe Mike didn't want to come."

Mike Wilson was her boyfriend of three years.

She waved her hand. "You know he has no taste in music. Even if he hadn't gone away with his family for the weekend, he wouldn't have showed. He would have been all about Paul's party."

"Well it is the 'party of the year,'" I said, making air quotes. At least that's what Paul and everyone else were calling it. Not that they weren't right. A party at the start of spring break our senior year, in Paul's giant town house while his parents were out, had the makings of an epic night. Although not as epic as this concert. *This* was everything.

"Thank you for skipping it to come here with me," Trina said.

"Are you kidding me? Like I'd miss this."

She shrugged. "Yeah, but Zev is Paul's cousin; I know he wanted you to be there."

"You and I have been planning tonight for ages. My boyfriend can handle the evening without me. No way I was going to cancel. This is our night. Besides, Zev's got me *all* week." I raised my eyebrows up and down. Tonight was just the start of my vacation, and if it was any indicator of what was to come, this was going to be a week I'd still be talking about when I was eighty.

She shook her head. "I still can't believe you convinced your parents to let you spend spring break in Florida with your boyfriend."

"Just call me the parent whisperer." Although we both knew that wasn't true. My parents could be a little helicopterish, which meant I had to fudge the truth here and there. In this instance, I told them I wanted to spend my vacation at my gram's in Florida. It wasn't until after I booked my nonrefundable flight that I let them know Zev was going to be spending the week down there, too. His grandparents lived about seven minutes away from my gram in Boca. My parents were less than thrilled with this development. But, hey, it wasn't my fault the area was basically a mecca for old people from Manhattan. At least that's how I explained it to them. They gave in. Probably figured I couldn't get into too much trouble while staying at a retirement village. I hoped to prove them wrong.

"We can still catch some of the party if we go now," Trina

offered. "Don't tell me you're not curious. You're always curious."

"Seriously, I'm fine with anything. It's totally up to you. We Are Now is performing next. They're pretty good."

Trina scrunched her nose. "They're okay. I'm just sick of them already. I don't know why they keep getting booked every single week. You should be up there."

"Tell me about it." I'd been leaving demo after demo for Sheila, the club's owner, but so far all I'd gotten was an *I'll let you know*. "We can do something else if you want. This night is all yours. You're the one stuck here all break."

"Yeah." Trina let out a sigh. "With my sister. Why does NYU have to have the same break as us?"

Her sister, Keisha, was a junior at New York University—the same school Trina had decided she'd go to next year—and she was driving Trina batty with her nonstop "college wisdom and experience." I would never tell Trina this, best-friend code and all meant I had to take her side 100 percent of the time, but I could see where Keisha was coming from. I'd probably do the same thing if my little brother wound up at the same school as me.

"Let's see how the party looks," Trina said, and pulled out her phone. She punched up GroupIt and scrolled through what seemed like a million photos. She froze and looked up at me. "You are not going to like this. At all. We should get to the party now."

I took a deep breath. "What is it?"

She turned the phone so I could get a clear look. "Bethanne is hanging all over Zev."

I let the air out. "Is that it? That's no surprise."

"Umm . . . why aren't you freaking out?" she asked. "You're the one who said she wants him back."

I shrugged. "I know, but he doesn't want her. I told Zev what she was up to and he swore up and down that they were just friends. I trust him."

Trina nodded. She knew how much he loved me. The guy was getting on an airplane for me tomorrow, and that was major. He had a *huge* flying phobia. Enough so that his family drove the last four times they went to Florida. That wasn't all. He brought my whole family chicken soup when we all caught the flu, he helped my brother with his bar mitzvah lessons, he listened to me practice guitar for hours just so he could spend more time with me, and he always put me first. There were a lot of things that I freaked out about, but Zev cheating was not one of them.

Trina went back to swiping. "It's still annoying," she said. "Look at this. It says she tagged Zev Geller in seven photos. I *really* can't stand her."

I rolled my eyes. She wasn't alone. Bethanne Dubois was not exactly my favorite person, either. I found her to be smug and obnoxious and that was before I started dating her ex. Not that I had anything to do with the breakup. She ended things with him the fall of sophomore year. Zev and I didn't even really know each other until we became juniors. We started dating that December. Obviously, I didn't love that Bethanne was making a play for him, even if Zev couldn't see it for what it was, but I knew it wasn't going to amount to anything. So if Zev wanted her as a friend, while I didn't quite understand it, I could live with it.

"I think we should go to the party," Trina said.

"Not if this is because of Bethanne," I told her.

"It's not. There are a ton of people there. And look." She pointed to another picture on her phone. "Trevor's there with his new boyfriend. He's been talking about him for weeks. I haven't met him yet. We're all going to prom together; it would be nice to get to know him beforehand, right?"

"Yeah." Although I wasn't positive that was her true motive, I was never one to pass up a good party. And even though I'd be seeing Zev tomorrow, the idea of hanging out with him tonight too made me smile. It would be the perfect end to a perfect night.

TWO

"You know you drive almost as bad as my gram," I told Trina once I was safely out of her car.

Paul had a totally sick town house. Unfortunately, it was out of the way of any public transportation and way too long of a walk.

"Which is why my parents like me to practice," she answered, matter-of-factly. Being in Manhattan, we didn't tend to drive much. My family didn't even have a car, but Trina's did. It primarily lived in a parking garage, but every so often one of them took it out. I wanted to take a cab to Paul's, but Trina insisted on driving. I knew my parents would have flipped, they were not fans of teen drivers, but I decided this was one of those things they didn't need to know about. After all, chances were good Trina had more skills behind the wheel than some of the cab drivers I'd ridden with. "And you are not one to talk," she pointed out.

"Very true." I didn't have a license. I hadn't even bothered taking driver's ed. I didn't have a car to practice with, I always planned on going to college in the city (and now that I got into the Manhattan School of Music, I was definitely sticking around), and there were enough cabs and car services to make it seem like a waste of time. Trina assured me I would regret the decision, but so far I hadn't.

"And did you see the way I nailed the parallel parking?" she said. "One shot. Right in."

"Very impressive," I told her. "Your keys," I said, pointing to the car.

"Oh yeah." Trina was the smartest person I knew, but could be completely absentminded when it came to the little stuff like locking doors or remembering to take her things. Although the car keys weren't entirely her fault. She was used to leaving them in the engine for the parking attendant. She grabbed the keys, clicked the locks shut, then struggled to fit the keychain into her wristlet.

"Give it to me," I said, and tossed it into my purse.

Trina traveled light. Phone, apartment key, credit card, license, a couple of bucks, and a lip gloss—that was it. Me on the other hand? My bag was a bottomless pit. It had everything: a notebook and pen to write down lyrics that popped into my head, Band-Aids, a flashlight, a glue stick, sunscreen, makeup, aspirin, an umbrella, a book, and a variety of other supplies— because you never know what you might need. I thought it was very Mary Poppins of me, but Zev joked it was like I was in training to be a *Let's Make a Deal* audience member. The show's host gave people money for having random things on them. But Zev could make fun all he wanted—he wasn't laughing when his pants split right before his improv show last month (okay, he kind of was) and I came to the rescue with a needle and thread.

"Kind of quiet for the party of the year," I said as we walked up the steps to Paul's.

"Maybe everyone left already." We got to the door. "Do I knock or just go in?" Trina asked.

I pressed my ear up and smiled as I made out the familiar beat to one of my favorite songs coming from inside. "They're still in there," I said, and tried the handle. It was open.

"Quick, shut the door!" someone yelled before we even fully stepped inside. It was our friend, Amy. "Sorry," she said, after we did as instructed. "One of the neighbors threatened to call the cops, so Paul put me on door duty."

A possible visit by the police? Paul's party could very well live up to the hype.

Trina tensed up. "I will be grounded for life if we get busted here."

Even though it was ages ago, her parents, *and* mine, were still pretty pissed over the fake ID thing.

"I think we'll be okay. Besides we're already here," I reminded her. Now that we were, I was kind of excited. It looked like the whole senior class and then some were crammed inside Paul's place. I didn't want to leave before we even got a chance to say hi to everyone. "Just one drink, maybe two, then we're out of here," I assured her.

She gave me a look. "Yeah, I know," I said. I always mean to just pop in and stay for fifteen minutes, but somehow, I always wind up being the last one to leave. "But this time I mean it." I held up three fingers. "Scouts honor. I have my flight tomorrow. I need some sleep."

Trina still looked skeptical.

"Besides," I said, "we didn't hear anything outside. As long as Amy keeps doing her job, we'll be fine. No one will call the cops."

"You're right," Trina said, her body relaxing. "And worst-case scenario, I guess a jail cell beats staying in my apartment with my sister."

I shook my head. "Come on," I said, taking her arm and pulling her through the crowd. I wanted to find Zev.

"Drinks are in the kitchen," Amy called after us.

We didn't make it that far, though. "You're here!" Trevor said, catching us midway. "I thought you had the concert?"

"We did and it was . . ." I gestured to show my head exploding. "We thought we'd finish up the night here."

"Nice." He introduced us to his new boyfriend, Dominick. The two met at an internship orientation for the city's Department of Design and Construction. Trevor was into the design aspect and Dom the engineering. When Trina heard that, I knew where the conversation was headed. The mere mention of anything STEM related was all it took to draw her in. My eyes glazed over as she and Dom threw around terms like *microscale sensors*, *fluidic systems*, and *MEMS*.

"Some of this will help," Trevor said, pointing to his drink.

"What is it?"

"A wide assortment of what I found lying around," he said, offering me the cup. "Want some?"

"Uhh, yeah." I winked at him and took a huge sip. Then I did everything possible not to spit it back in the cup. "Oh my God. That was disgusting."

Trevor laughed. "Maybe not my best creation, but I worked with what I had. There's beer in the kitchen. And I think you'll find something else you'll like in there."

"Zev?"

"At least as of a few minutes ago."

"Then I will be right back. Anybody else want anything?" I asked.

They all shook their head. Trina rarely drank and never when she was driving.

"Sari!" my physics partner Jeremy said when I entered the kitchen. "Want?" he asked, holding up a beer.

I nodded.

"Catch."

"No!" I yelled, moving closer. The chances of the bottle actually landing in my hands were about as good as Kevin Wayward materializing in a burst of smoke. Probably worse.

"Thanks," I said, taking the drink from him. "Have you seen Zev?"

I couldn't wait to tell him all about the concert.

"Over by the fridge, last I saw," Jeremy said.

"'K, I'll be right back." After listening to all those Kevin Wayward songs, no one could possibly blame me for wanting to snuggle up beside my boyfriend. Some of those songs were seriously hot.

I squeezed through a couple of people to try to get to the other side of the room. Zev was the tallest guy in our class, so he'd be easy to find. I thought I spotted the back of his head, but the guy in front of me was blocking my view.

"Excuse me," I said.

He moved a little, and I got a better look at that floppy, dark hair. It was Zev!

I moved closer and was about to call out to him, but his name got stuck in my throat.

He wasn't alone.

He was with Bethanne.

But they weren't just standing there. Zev's mouth was attached to hers. They were *kissing*.

Everything seemed to happen so slow and so fast at the same time. I gasped and the bottle slipped from my hand, shattering at my feet. Kind of like my life.

Images and sounds swirled around me. Someone asking me if I was okay, the whispering and ogling from my classmates, and then, of course, Zev. He turned and caught my eye. His mouth was agape and his expression one of panic.

"Sari, it's not—"

I didn't wait for an explanation. I just ran. There was nothing he could say. I pushed through the crowd until I was outside. I heard Amy yell to shut the door, but I didn't care. I just needed to get away. Away from the memory of the guy I loved kissing someone else. Of his lips, those soft lips that were supposed to be mine, touching Bethanne. Away from the image of the two of them pressed up against each other. I had been so stupid to believe nothing was going on between them. Now I knew the truth, even though part of me wished I didn't. And away from the reality that Zev and I were no longer *Zev and I*.

But no matter how far I ran, I couldn't erase the hurt I was feeling.

THREE

Somehow I'd made it down the steps and partway up the
street. I felt the urge to collapse right onto the ground, but
there was no way I was going to let that happen. I wiped away
tears with the back of my hand, but more just kept coming. I
needed to pull it together. Zev couldn't be too far behind me,
and he was not going to see what a mess he turned me into. No
way I was giving him that satisfaction. I needed a place to hide.
Quickly.

Paul's street and the surrounding ones were residential.
Why couldn't he live near a bodega or a twenty-four-hour CVS
like the rest of Manhattan? There was nothing but town houses,
apartment buildings, trees, and cars around here.

Cars. I had access to one of them.

I fished through my bag until I found Trina's key chain. I
pushed the button to unlock the car, and the alarm wailed.

Crap. I had no idea how to turn this thing off. I looked back
at the door. Still no sign of Zev, but who knew how much time
I had? Probably not long. I kept hitting the button. The noise
finally stopped. I opened the door, got in the backseat, locked
myself in, and let my head rest on the seat.

I so wanted this to be a dream. One that I'd wake up from any second. Only I knew that wasn't the case. Zev cheated on me. It was hard to believe, but I saw it with my own eyes. Not just me. Jeremy, Chaya, Seth, Tova, everyone in that kitchen. Zev didn't even care that the whole school would be gossiping about how poor Sari got dumped in the most brutal way possible. I didn't even want to think about the looks of pity they'd be giving me.

"Sari! Where are you? Sari!"

My body went still at the sound of Zev's voice. I squeezed my eyes shut and prayed he didn't find me.

"Sari!" he called again. I used to love the way he said my name, now it made my chest hurt. "Sari!" His voice was getting closer. I hoped he didn't recognize Trina's car. He'd only ridden in it a handful of times. I curled up into the tiniest ball I could manage.

Another pair of footsteps ran over. "Just go, Zev." It was Trina. Hearing her voice only made me cry harder.

"I need to talk to her," he said.

"You did enough," she told him. "I've got this."

"No, I need to explain."

"No, you need to go." Her voice was seething. "I'm serious, Zev. Get of here. Now. She'll talk to you when she wants to."

A few seconds, a minute, an hour went by. I couldn't tell. It felt like an eternity, but was probably mere moments. Time always seemed slower when you didn't want it to be. There was a light knock on the window. "Sari," Trina said.

I didn't look up. "Are you alone?"

"Yes," she answered softly.

I clicked the button on the key chain, and slid over to make room for her as she got into the car beside me.

She put her hand on my back. "I'm so sorry."

My whole body convulsed and tears poured out of me. Not the quiet sobs from before, but loud, raw ones. The type you'd never see on TV because they're red faced, snot filled, and ugly. Trina leaned down, her body on mine, and she wrapped her arms around me. "We'll get through this," she said. "We'll get through this."

Then she just let me cry it out.

A few minutes after my wails turned back to silent tears, I sat up.

"I wish I had a tissue for you," she said.

"I have one in there." I gestured toward my purse on the floor.

She smiled at me and handed me my bag. "Of course you do."

I took one out and looked at my reflection in the rearview mirror. I was a mess. The giant top bun I had so carefully pinned up earlier was coming undone, with random strands of wavy, golden-brown hair sticking out in every direction. My eyes were red rimmed and glossy. The tears made them a brighter blue than usual. I would have liked the color under different circumstances. My makeup was frightening. Black streaks went all the way to my chin. If I was auditioning for the part of a serial killer in a horror film, I'd probably have gotten it. I didn't even bother trying to wipe it off. I just blew my nose. It was fitting that I looked as bad as I felt.

"So you heard what happened?" I asked.

Trina nodded.

"Everyone knows?" I was pretty sure of the answer, but I needed to know for sure.

She nodded again.

"I'm so stupid," I said.

"No, you're not."

Yeah, I was. I had fallen for every line Zev Geller had ever fed me.

"Sari, he's the idiot. Not you. You deserve better."

I reached for another tissue and saw my phone blowing up. Zev's name and a picture of us at the junior prom appeared on the screen. "Guess who it is?" I said while hitting Decline.

There were four missed calls and seven texts.

"Maybe you should talk to him," Trina suggested. "See what he has to say?"

I shook my head. "I want nothing to do with him." Another text popped up, and I deleted it along with every other message he ever sent me. There was no coming back from this. It was better to just cut it off cold turkey.

My phone rang again.

Trina looked at me. "I'll be really quiet if you want to answer it."

I shook my head.

I turned off the ringer, but I could still see Zev's name popping up. He just kept calling. "Seriously!" I said, throwing the phone down on the seat between Trina and me. "He needs to stop. I can't deal with this right now. I can't talk to him. I can't even say his name. It hurts to just look at it."

Trina picked up the phone. "Then *He-Who-Must-Not-Be-Named* is history," she said and changed Zev's contact information to read *Voldemort*.

"Thanks."

She put her arm around me. "I'm here for you. Anything you need."

"Want to take my place on a trip to Florida tomorrow?" I threw my head back against the seat. "How am I going to survive that? The flight. The *car ride*. It's going to be hell. His *parents* are picking me up tomorrow and driving us to the airport."

"Not anymore," she said. "They were supposed to pick you up at eleven, right?"

I nodded.

"Well, I'm picking you up at eight. We'll get you to the airport super early and see if you can get a standby flight. Then you won't even have to see him."

"Yeah?"

"Yeah," she said.

This could work. A week sulking in Florida definitely beat a week sulking in New York with my parents asking a million questions.

"I still need to—"

She put up her hand. "I will contact *Voldemort* and let him know you no longer need a ride," she said, reading my mind.

"Thank you."

"It's what best friends are for. Now please tell me you have a makeup wipe in that bag of yours," she said, looking inside it. "Your mother will freak if she sees you like this."

She found one and handed it to me.

"Seriously," I said, putting my head on her shoulder. "I don't know what I'd do without you."

"Lucky for you," she said, "you never have to find out."

Even with everything that had just happened, I actually smiled. I might have had lousy taste when it came to picking a boyfriend, but my choice in a best friend was on point.

FOUR

"Sari, is that you?" my dad asked as I opened the door.

I had really hoped he'd be asleep, but I should have known better. My parents never went to bed until my little brother, Dan, and I were home and safely in our rooms for the night.

"Yep," I called out to him, "see you in the morning."

"What? No good night?"

I took a deep breath, stepped into the living room, and braced for an inquisition. It wasn't just Dad in there. It was Mom, too. *Perfect.*

She dog-eared the page in her book and gave me her undivided attention. "How was the concert?"

"Good."

"That's it?" my dad asked. "You talked about this concert for weeks, begged us to let you stay out, and all we get is 'good'?"

"Really good," I said. "Amazing."

I knew I was fortunate to have parents who cared and wanted to know what was going on in my life, but right now a tiny bit of apathy would have been greatly appreciated. I just wanted to hide under the covers and pretend this night never happened. Answering questions was about the last thing I wanted to do.

My mom's eyes zeroed in on me. "Are you okay?"

I felt myself squirm under her gaze. "Yeah."

"Have you been crying?"

Why did she have to be so observant? "It's just really hot out." That part was true. We'd been having freakishly warm weather for this time of year. "My makeup practically melted."

Now both of my parents were studying me.

"I'm fine, really."

"Sari, what's wrong?" my dad asked.

I wasn't getting out of there without giving them something. "Zev and I got in a fight. It's nothing," I lied. I didn't feel like going into the whole thing right now. I couldn't, not without having another breakdown. It didn't help that my parents loved Zev and would be disappointed, too.

My mom came over and kissed the top of my head. "I'm sure you two will work it out. You have the whole ride to the airport, and the flight to talk things out."

"Yeah," I said. "Speaking of tomorrow. I'm going to get up early and meet Trina for breakfast and go to the airport from there. Zev knows where I'll be." I didn't want to risk telling my parents the truth. If they knew Trina was taking me to catch an early flight, there was a good chance they'd veto the idea.

My mom pursed her lips together. I knew she was hoping to have a "family" morning before I went away for the week, but I'd have been lousy company anyway. There was no way I'd get through breakfast pretending everything was all platinum-record-and-Grammy-winning-dream worthy. Besides, this was good practice for them for when college started, and I wouldn't be around as much.

My little brother appeared from his room. "Why did you guys force me go to bed if you were going to keep me up with all your talking?" he asked.

"Sorry," my dad told him. "We'll be quieter."

Dan to the rescue. I decided to use that as my way out.

"Can I go to bed now, too?" I asked.

My parents were still scrutinizing me, but finally said okay after I promised to give them a proper good-bye in the morning.

I plugged my phone in to charge and rested it on my suitcase so I wouldn't forget it tomorrow. Trina's talk with Zev hadn't stopped him from trying to get in touch with me. There were twenty-two texts from Voldemort waiting for me. The latest message was still visible on my screen.

VOLDEMORT
Please, Sari.

Please what? Ignore the fact that he was a cheating jerk who broke my heart? I didn't need more of his lies. I erased all the texts again and kicked the suitcase. It was a painful reminder of everything that happened. I had been so excited for this trip. I thought it was going to bring us even closer. What a pathetic, lovesick dork I had been.

Tears filled my eyes again. How was I supposed to get over him? I sat back on my bed. I had never felt this empty before. Not when I got passed over for the lead in *Little Shop of Horrors*, not when I got kicked off marching band for missing too many practices (I was more focused on my guitar work than on my drumming and moving in formation, but I really wanted to do both), not even in the eighth grade when Quinn Ridely (Bethanne's best friend) posted a picture on GroupIt of my head superimposed on Jabba the Hutt's body and wrote "Only a slight improvement." All those things seemed like nothing compared to the pain I was feeling now.

I reached for my guitar, Ruby, carefully pulling her out of the case. Touching the small red jewel I'd stuck on the front as a child, I couldn't help but smile a bit through my tears. Some things were a constant, like me and Ruby. Looked like we'd be spending a lot of time together this week. More than usual. I've heard pain is great material for songwriting, maybe this would be the silver lining to this whole disaster.

I grimaced at the saying. *Silver lining.* My dad used that all the time, a silly family joke, and I'd always roll my eyes. But now I needed it to be true.

I let out a deep breath. I was going to make something happen on this trip. I was going to take my music to the next level. I didn't need Zev to make me happy. I'd be perfectly fine all by myself.

I grabbed my phone and punched up Voldemort's name and typed: *We're over.*

My eyes lingered on the words. They stung, but I hit Send anyway.

He hadn't given me any choice; not after what he'd done.

Zev and I were officially through.

FIVE

Together Trina and I pulled my suitcase from the trunk of her car. It weighed a ton. I had *slightly* overpacked. When I was throwing everything in, I wasn't exactly sure what Zev and I would be doing, so I wanted to make sure I had all my options covered. There were formal dresses, casual-chic looks, and comfy but cute sportswear. I could have pulled most of the stuff out, I really only wanted sweats and T-shirts now, but I couldn't bring myself to go through it all. So I just lugged it with me. It may not have been the wisest choice.

"Now you remember what you have to do?" she asked.

"Trina."

"Don't Trina me. Repeat it back. Rule one."

I shook my head. "I am not doing that."

She put her hands on her hips. "There is no better way to get over a guy than by finding another one, and you'll be in Florida during spring break. I expect detailed stories when you return."

"I'll be at a retirement community. I don't think I'll be finding the type of guys you're envisioning, not unless there's a time machine involved." Not that I even wanted to meet someone new. Obviously, I couldn't sulk over Zev forever, but it had only been a day. I wasn't ready to move on. Not yet. Not even close.

"Well, you have to keep to rule number two, at least."

"That's a given." Rule Two was that we had to talk/text every day. "When have I ever slacked on that?"

She smirked. "Eighth grade."

"That was not my fault." In the seven years we'd been BFFs we'd gone only five days without communicating, and that was just because my parents confiscated my phone and grounded me from the computer, TV, and every other electronic device. I had *allegedly* stolen Quinn's top while she was showering after gym class and replaced it with a handcrafted extra-long T-shirt that read: I'M MEAN BECAUSE I'M INSECURE. The back said: & BECAUSE I HAVE A STICK UP MY BUTT. There was even a little be-dazzled staff and butt crack.

Somehow the fire alarm went off right then resulting in her having to go and stand in front of the whole school in her new attire. I put on a Jabba the Hutt T-shirt as I walked outside. When I passed her, I said, "I think you forgot that before Luke Skywalker, Jabba destroyed his enemies. I'd call us even now." I totally got suspended, but it was worth it.

"I'm going to miss you," Trina said.

"Me too, but we're going to be talking so much you won't even realize I'm gone."

I got my knapsack from the backseat and threw it over my shoulder, and Trina handed me my guitar case and a little bag from Andrea's, our favorite bakery in the whole city.

"It's a surprise for on the plane, if you get upset or sad or even stuck on your original flight. It's totally better than He-Who-Must-Not-Be-Named."

"You didn't have to do this."

She shrugged. "I wanted to. Should I wait and see if you get standby?"

I shook my head. "You better get going. That traffic agent is shooting us death glares." I gave her a hug, as best I could with all my stuff, thanked her for everything, and then watched her drive off.

It was just me now.

I rolled my suitcase through the automatic doors. This was definitely not the trip I had been planning. The airport was busy, but it wasn't packed like I had expected. In fact, most people were using the self-serve check-in. There were only two people in line for the counter. I got to the front in minutes.

"Let me see," the agent said, after I asked if there were any earlier flights I could get on. "There's actually a seat left on a flight boarding in thirty minutes. You'll have to hurry."

I checked my bag and rushed to security. This was going to be cutting it close, but to my surprise I actually made it through the line and screening quickly. Something in my life was finally going right. I didn't know what was with all those people who complained about flying; this was great. After I made my way through, I slipped my shoes back on and ran to the gate.

I got there right as they called my zone to board. Did I mention how much I love the airport?

I walked down the aisle to my row and spotted an empty overhead bin above my seat. I didn't even have to search for a place to fit my guitar. *Thank you.* The airport gods were smiling on me.

I moved into my window seat and fastened my seat belt, squishing myself as far over to the wall as I could. I did not want my hips spilling over into the seat next to me. Economy airport seating was not exactly designed for people with curves in mind, and I certainly had my share of them. My mom joked that the women in our family got in line twice when they were handing out hips and chests. I had a few extra pounds thrown in to keep them company.

Ninety percent of the time, I was cool with that. Dealing with airplane, theater, bus, and subway seats contributed to the other ten.

A woman about my mother's age moved into the spot next to me. To my relief her hips were half the size of mine, so I didn't have to worry about brushing up against her the whole flight. She barely acknowledged me, but I didn't care. I wasn't exactly in the mood for chitchat anyway. I reached into my backpack and pulled out my earbuds and phone.

Right before I put the phone on airplane mode, I made the mistake of checking GroupIt. It felt like someone stabbed me with an icicle when I saw my profile pic. I hadn't taken down the one of Zev and me. We were cute together, height difference and all. I just hit five feet while he was six four—although he was only six one when we started dating. And his look. I was a sucker for it. Nerdy hot. Lanky with shaggy dark-brown hair and black rectangular glasses. And Zev just always seemed at ease. It was reassuring.

Stop it, Sari. I didn't need to be thinking about his attributes. I switched my photo to one of me performing in the school talent show. Music was my true love. Zev had only been a distraction.

I grabbed the bag from Andrea's Bakery and pulled out the contents. Yes! Trina got me a do'wich. My favorite dessert in the entire universe: a glazed donut with dark-chocolate ganache, sliced in half, with chocolate hazelnut mousse on the inside surrounded by crushed Oreo. Totally decadent.

The woman next to me gave me a judgy look.

I was not putting up with it. Not today. "What?" I asked, ready to fire back with a scathing retort to the predictable "should you really be eating that" comment. I mean hello, it was a donut sandwich. *Nobody* "should" be eating it. But what I put in my mouth was nobody's business.

"Sorry," she said, "I've never seen one of those. It looks amazing."

Oh. Okay, I was jumping to conclusions, looking for a fight. Zev wasn't there, so random strangers were bearing the brunt of it. Anger was the second stage of grief, after all. I just wanted to be at acceptance already.

"Take this," I said, holding out half of my do'wich. It came precut.

She looked skeptical.

"Seriously," I said, trying to show her I wasn't a grouchy seatmate. "My grandmother will shoot me if I show up having already eaten. You'll be doing me a favor."

She took it from me. *Good.* Nice deeds and acts of kindness would help me get rid of the anger. Well, maybe.

I went back to GroupIt and pulled up Zev's page. I immediately unfriended him. Unfortunately, he kept all his pictures and posts public, so I could still see everything.

"Who's that?" the woman next to me asked. "Boyfriend? He's handsome. Kind eyes."

More like deceiving ones.

Gorgeous, though. The hazel color always drew me in, but it

was really his smile and that little dimple just below his right eye and above the apple of his cheek that accompanied it that made me melt.

"He's nobody," I said, more trying to convince myself than her.

Only he wasn't nobody. He was a guy who chose to go to Columbia next year instead of Penn just so he'd be closer to me. Why would he do that if he didn't care? Maybe . . . maybe there was a chance for us.

I had to stop thinking like this. There was no going soft. Zev was bad news. I couldn't trust him, and I valued myself more than staying with someone like that.

I just needed a reminder. I clicked on the pictures he was tagged in, so I could see him standing there, all cozy with Bethanne. The stabbing feeling inside me returned, but that was okay. I needed it. I needed to remember that he hurt me and I should hate him.

I wanted to hate her, too. To call her names, refer to her as a cross between a Muppet and a troll. But she wasn't. She was beautiful. Tall, lithe. They made a striking couple. Yeah, Bethanne may have stolen my boyfriend, but this wasn't on her. It was on Zev. *He* was the one I trusted. *He* was the one who broke his word. *He* was the one I counted on. If she could just take him away like that, I didn't really want him anyway. At least that's what I had to keep telling myself.

I put my earbuds in, turned on some Kevin Wayward, put my head back, and closed my eyes. Apparently, Zev never got over his first love. Hopefully I wouldn't have the same problem.

SIX

I opened the screen door and poked my head into Gram's place. "Hello."

"Sari!" she said, coming out of the kitchen, wiping her hands on a towel. "I'm supposed to be picking you up in a few hours."

"I caught an early flight and took a car here. Thought I'd surprise you."

She engulfed me in a giant hug. The familiar scent of lavender and vanilla wafted over me. Coming here already felt like the right decision.

Gram took a step back and looked me over, her hands still on my shoulders. "As beautiful as ever. And where's that boy of yours?" She gave me a squeeze. "You may have fooled your mom, but your gram knows the real reason you're here."

When I didn't answer, she winked at me. "Don't worry, I'm not mad. I'll take any excuse to spend more time with you."

Gram took my hand and led me into the living room. She sat on the couch and patted the seat next to her. "So where is he?" she persisted. "When do I get to say hello?"

I studied the dark veins in her soft beige wood flooring. "You don't. We broke up."

"Oh, Sari. I'm so sorry. What happened?" she asked.

"He . . . he . . ." I couldn't say it. I just shook my head.

She didn't press. Instead she clapped her hands together. "Okay, let's take your mind off things. Want to bake? Go shopping? We can stop by those massage chairs at that electronic store you like—Jordan's."

"Nah." I took my shoes off and pulled my knees closer to me.

"We can go to a real spa," she offered. "Wouldn't that be nice? A massage, a mani-pedi. I haven't had one of those in ages."

"I'm not really in the mood." Just talking about Zev put me back in my funk. Going out seemed like so much effort, and I just got there.

"What about a movie? A bunch of new comedies just came out. Seems like you could use a laugh."

"I don't know." Now that I was on the couch, I really didn't feel like moving. I liked my little curled-up ball. "Maybe we can watch one here?"

And that's what we did. Over the next several days I watched three movies (specifically ones that were romance free), binged two seasons of a ridiculous supernatural thriller that I couldn't turn away from despite (or maybe because of) the campiness, and caught every daytime game show that came on the air. By Tuesday, Gram had had enough.

"No more sulking," she said, batting my feet off the couch and onto the floor. "It's time for you to work on healing. You haven't been outside since you got here. You haven't even picked up your guitar."

To my disappointment, pain hadn't turned me into a focused, productive human being. It had made me a couch potato with a serious lack of motivation. "I know. I'm pathetic. I'm sorry."

"Hey," she put her hand on my chin and lifted it so my head was held high. "Do not talk about my granddaughter that way. You, Sari Silver, come from a long line of strong women. You are smart, talented, beautiful, kind—don't let one foolish boy bring you down. You had your mourning time, now it's time to rise up. There are amazing things ahead. Now let me hear it."

"Gram . . ."

"Come on," she insisted.

"*I am capable, confident, and can do whatever I put my mind to,*" I recited with a roll of my eyes. It was kind of her mantra, and when I was little, whenever I was feeling down, she made me say it. I was surprised it took her 'til Tuesday to drag it out.

"Nope," she said. "I want it with feeling. Convince me you believe it."

"Gram."

"Humor an old lady."

"Fine."

I said her mantra again.

She made me do it five more times before she finally let me off the hook. "That's my girl," she said, with a smile.

As corny as it sounded, it actually made me feel a little better. I smiled back at her.

"Now," she continued, reaching for the remote and shutting the TV off, "this complex has a wonderful pool. Take your guitar, notebook, whatever. Go swim, go play music, go write—anything but more TV."

She was right, it was about time I did something. I got in my bathing suit and studied myself in the mirror. Back at home I'd gone to eight stores hunting for the perfect beachwear. When I found this one, I was so excited. It had a retro vibe and highlighted everything I wanted highlighted. It accentuated my waist and chest, and was even emerald green—Zev's favorite color. He would have gone crazy seeing me in this. *Stop it*, I reminded myself yet again. It didn't matter what Zev would have liked. *I* liked the suit—that's what counted.

I pulled my hair back into a low pony. It went down to just about my belly button. Maybe I'd get a trim when I got back to New York, or just chop it all off and go for a whole new look. You know, embrace change.

I grabbed my stuff—my guitar, towel, bag, and phone—and headed to the pool. I wasn't sure I wanted to actually swim, but at least I could get some sun. Gram decided to stay home and make her famous peanut butter cookies, so I took the opportunity to call Trina away from prying ears on my walk over.

It would be nice to have something besides TV recaps and sob stories about Zev to talk about.

"Hang on," I told Trina as I got to the pool. "I need both hands to open the gate." I tucked the phone between my ear and shoulder and managed to maneuver it. "I'm back. And I'm in."

"Is it old-person central?" she asked. "Gray hair as far as the eye can see?"

It actually wasn't that crowded. Three people around Gram's age were sitting on beach chairs chatting. That was it. The pool was empty.

Or at least it had appeared that way.

A second later, someone emerged from underwater.

"Oh my God," I said, doing a double take.

"What?" Trina asked. "Old guys in bathing suits? Be nice. Don't forget, we'll be old too someday."

"No, that's not it."

She couldn't be more wrong.

The guy in the pool was *young*.

And *hot*.

And tan.

And dripping wet.

With the biggest muscles I'd ever seen in real life. If I didn't know better, I would have thought Trina had planted him there.

"What is going on?" she asked.

"Captain America is in the pool," I whispered.

"The actor?!"

"No, but someone who looks just like him."

"This," she said, "is what I'm talking about. Time to make some spring break memories. He can be your rebound. Go dive in. Tell him you're not a good swimmer and may need mouth-to-mouth."

"Trina . . ."

"Or," she went on, "is there a hot tub? Ask him to join you. Tell him you want to make it really steamy, and can't do it without him, and does he have any idea of how to turn up the heat."

"You read too much smut," I told her.

"You call it smut, I call it a how-to guide," she said. "One you'd be a fool not to follow."

"I'm hanging up on you now."

"I want pictures . . . and details. Don't disappoint me," she said.

"Good-bye, Trina."

I hung up, and actually considered if there was a way I could snap a shot without seeming totally skeevy, but the next thing I knew the guy was back underwater. I watched as he moved; every part of him was so chiseled.

My mouth dropped slightly when I realized he was swimming in my direction. Before I had a chance to move, he popped up at the side of the pool. He looked up at me with the biggest brown eyes imaginable.

"It's not cold," he said, "I promise."

"Huh?"

"The water."

Oh yeah. Why was I having a problem thinking straight?

"Are you coming in?" he asked.

I was pretty sure it was his six-pack that was interfering with my mental capacity. I didn't even normally go for muscles. Zev was super lanky. *Ugh*. Why did my mind have to flash to my ex? I needed him out of my thoughts. I knew what Trina would suggest.

"Well?" Captain America asked.

I took a step closer to the pool.

Maybe it wouldn't hurt to get my feet wet, after all.

SEVEN

"I'll be right in," I told Captain America with a wink. I immediately did an about-face and headed for one of the nearby tables. I dropped my stuff down and rested my palms against the warm plastic.

What was I doing?! Did I really just wink at him? Despite what Trina suggested, I couldn't just move on. I didn't want a rebound. I wanted . . . I wanted what I'd had, but that was impossible. It'd been destroyed. I just needed to relax. This was only a swim. No biggie. I turned back to the pool.

He was watching me. This was insane. There were not supposed to be hot boys here. This was a *retirement community*. But since he was looking, I figured I might as well put on a show— make Trina proud.

I slowly walked, you could even say I sauntered, over to the diving board. I got to the end, bent my knees, jumped into the air, arms extended, and executed what I would call an award-worthy dive. Not even a splash when I hit the water.

"Nice," he said.

"Thank you." He was about eight feet away, but I didn't

make a move to get any closer. I stayed where I was, treading water.

It didn't take long for him to make his way to me.

"I'm Fitz," he said, holding out his fist.

Was I supposed to bump it? Did people still do that? "I'm Sari," I said, tapping my knuckles to his. "You seem a little young for this place."

I realized our hands were still touching, and I quickly dropped mine back into the water.

"Visiting my grandpa," he said. "You?"

"Same. Well, grandma."

A cloud passed overhead, clearing the way to let the sun beat down on us. Fitz leaned back, his head grazing the water, soaking it in. He rubbed his hand through his short, spiky blond hair and took a deep breath and let it out slowly. He did it three times. I wasn't sure if it was for my benefit or if he was just super chi or something.

"So," I said after what seemed like forever passed. "Do you live around here?"

If Fitz was feeling the same awkwardness that I was, he didn't show it. He lifted his head back up, and looked me right in the eyes. "L.A., but I go to school in New York."

I raised an eyebrow at him. "I'm from New York. Where do you go?"

"NYU." His gaze was getting stronger, if that was even possible. The guy had some serious eye contact going on.

He didn't say anything else, so I felt the need to fill in the silence. I started talking about Trina going there next year and asking if he knew Keisha. He didn't. Then I just offered up that

I was a senior and was going to be studying music in the city next year.

"So the guitar's not just a hobby?" he asked, cocking his head toward my instrument.

"No, it's kind of my life."

"Respect," he said and put his fist out again.

Who was this guy?

He seemed so chill. Zev had a relaxed demeanor to him, but he also was full of energy. Quick on his feet, always ready with a comeback or encouraging word or biting remark depending on the situation. Fitz on the other hand seemed to almost float through a conversation. He definitely did not seem like most people I knew in the city.

"Why NYU?" I asked him.

"Followed a girl. Didn't work out; we broke up. But, hey, things happen for a reason, right?"

"Hope so." I also hoped that one day I'd be as nonchalant talking about the end of my relationship.

"No, it does. Because of her, I started volunteering at an after-school program for at-risk teens. I love it. Teach them tai chi, boxing, help them with homework. I'm majoring in childhood education now. Before I'd planned on doing nutrition and dietetics. Changed my whole path."

"Wow." I wondered what my life would be like now if I had never met Zev. I probably would have still been in marching band. He was part of the reason I was always late to practice. But then again, maybe I wouldn't have gotten into the Manhattan School of Music without him. He encouraged me to work on my songs all the time. Who knows; maybe everything would have been the same, well except for the heartache he caused.

Fitz splashed some water at me. "Hey, you okay? Didn't mean to stress you out."

"You didn't." I splashed him back.

"Good," he said. He sent another stream of water my way. "I like the whole philosophical what-if stuff." The cadence of his voice was slow and even. It was almost trancelike. "But my little sister says it makes me seem like a new-age hippie or like I belong to a cult."

"She should meet my brother," I offered. "That's a compliment compared to some of the things he's called me."

He threw more water in my direction, and I upped the ante. I jumped forward, kicking my feet so that waves would hit him.

He started laughing. "Is that how you want to play?" He dove, and the next thing I knew, he was beneath me, lifting me out of the water.

"Oh my God! Put me down." I was full-on laughing and screaming.

"Okay, but remember you asked."

Then he threw me back in the water.

"Oh, no you didn't," I said when I got back up, then I put my arm under the water, pushing it in his direction with all my might.

It was the move that may have officially launched our splash war. We were bobbing up and down, flinging water at each other, and dodging out of the way of attacks, all at the same time. The only downside was I was laughing so hard, that I gulped down what was probably an equivalent of a gallon of pool water.

"Watch it," one of the women at the table snapped after we'd gotten her wet.

"Sorry!" Fitz called out before turning back to me. "Can't have you assaulting poor little old ladies." He went to grab me.

"Oh, no you don't," I said, jumping up and trying to push him down into the water. He was strong. I wound up clinging to his back, my arms wrapped around his shoulders, pulling with all my might, but I couldn't get him to fall backward. He turned to face me, and I caught his eyes. They were nice eyes. *Really* nice eyes. But my stomach sank. They were nice, but they weren't Zev's.

"Truce, truce," I said, holding up my hands and floating away from him a little. This had been a nice distraction, but that's all it was. His wasn't the body I wanted pressed up against mine, despite how amazing it was. I would move on from Zev, I knew that, but not this quickly.

We got out of the pool and laid down on two beach chairs next to each other and just talked. A friend I could handle. He told me more about his after-school program, and NYU, and about skipping out on the Bahamas with some of his friends so he could save some money and because he worried his grandpa was lonely. Fitz's grandma passed away last year. I told him about school, and my dreams of being a singer, and that money (or lack thereof) was an issue for me, too, and how I had no idea what I was doing for the summer. I left out any mention of Zev, but Fitz could probably sense something was up. A lot of my stories had conspicuous gaps when you left Zev out of them.

I glanced at my phone. We'd been out there for over an hour. "I should get going," I said, "see what my grandma is up to."

"We should hang out tomorrow," Fitz offered. "I didn't even get to hear you play your guitar."

I liked hanging out with him, but—and I knew Trina would

say I was crazy—I kind of wanted time to myself. Not to sit and sulk, but to work on my music and, frankly, just to figure things out. Everything was going to be different now. "I think tomorrow is my grandma day," I said.

"Totally," he said. "But if you change your mind . . ." He put out his hand for my phone, and I gave it to him. He typed in his number and handed it back. "It's under Fitz."

I got up to leave, and he put out his hand for another fist bump.

This time I didn't hesitate. He really was a nice guy. Maybe he *was* Captain America, because he'd done something monumental, something only a hero could do. For a short while, he'd helped me to actually have a good time. I smiled my whole walk home. Until I got to Gram's front door.

Standing there with a bouquet of flowers was Zev.

EIGHT

Zev was there. At Gram's. Waiting for me.

Oh, please no.

I pulled my towel tighter around me like a cocoon. I wished it would swallow me up until he was out of my sight.

I didn't say anything, I just pushed past him.

"Sari, wait. Please."

I stopped just shy of the door, my back to him. "You shouldn't be here."

"You haven't answered any of my texts or calls. I had to try something."

"Or you could have taken a hint. I obviously don't want anything to do with you." I braced myself against the side of the condo just in case my knees buckled.

He ignored my comment. "I brought you these." He held out a bouquet of light-pink peonies. My favorite.

I willed myself not to cry. "I don't want them. I don't want anything from you."

"We can work this out, Sari. We're meant to be together." He put his hand on my shoulder, and I flinched.

I turned back to face him. "It doesn't work like that, Zev. You can't just get me flowers and expect everything to be okay. This isn't a rom-com, you can't buy my forgiveness, you can't play a song outside of my window or do some half-baked gesture and have me fall into your arms. This is bigger than that."

"I know."

I took a step back and looked up at him. He still towered over me, yet somehow didn't look tall. And his eyes. They were sunken and red. Had he been crying, too? I felt that now all-too-familiar tightness in my chest. I was about to bawl again. I needed to get away from him. "You should go."

"I want to talk. Please. I love you, Sari. I just want to explain."

"And I just wanted a boyfriend I could trust. We don't always get what we want." I ran into the condo and slammed the door shut behind me.

My grandmother was standing there, probably had been watching the whole thing. "Are you okay?" she asked.

I nodded. "I will be."

I picked up my phone and texted Fitz. *Guess what? I actually do have some time tomorrow. Let's hang out!*

NINE

"You should definitely kiss Fitz," Trina told me for the ump-teenth time since Zev showed up at my door yesterday. "It will make you feel better."

I doubted that. I was already second-guessing my decision to hang out with him at all. "It's not fair to use him as a rebound."

"Trust me, he won't mind."

But I would. "I told you," I said, switching the phone to my other ear. "This is just a friendly hangout with the only other person my age around here."

Well, close to my age. Trina did some digging after I told her about him, and if engineering didn't work out for her, detective work certainly would. With just the name Fitz, NYU, his major, and the after-school program he volunteered at, she was able to get the dirt on him. Cameron "Fitz" Fitzberg was a junior, a black belt in jujitsu, liked to surf, rock climb, and meditate in the park. At least that's what Trina got from his GroupIt page. He had more friends there than the two of us combined—and that was saying something. Her sister, Keisha, didn't know him from school, but after getting a look at his pictures, she wanted to.

"A wasted opportunity," Trina said. "I beg you to reconsider." When I didn't respond, she changed the subject. "Any more surprise visits from Voldemort? Or did you vanquish him?"

The texts hadn't stopped (although I still refused to read them), but at least he hadn't returned in person. "I—"

"Sari," my gram interrupted. "It's your mom."

"Can I call her back?"

"She says it's important."

I had been putting off talking to her. I sent a few texts but ignored the calls. Even when she'd reach out to Gram, I'd find an excuse not to get on the line. I'd have Gram tell her I said hi and that I sent my love. I just didn't want to answer questions about Zev, but it seemed like it was time for the inevitable. I told Trina I'd call her later and took the phone from Gram.

"Hi, Mom."

As expected, I got a mini guilt trip about not calling or answering the phone.

"I know Gram told you that Zev and I ended things," I explained, "and I wasn't in the mood to talk about it. I'm still not."

I knew she was concerned and wanted to know what was going on, but talking to her about it was harder than talking to Trina. I didn't want to break down again. I hadn't cried yet today, and I wanted to keep that streak going.

She didn't press. "That's not why I'm calling," she said. "It's about the weather."

I did my best to suppress a groan.

My mother was *obsessed* with the weather. Seriously. She'd actually flip channels to compare what was being said on each station. And the way she talked about Audrey Puente, one of the Fox 5 meteorologists, you'd think the two were best friends. "Audrey said this . . . Audrey said that . . ." And it wasn't just Audrey. Any time Mike Woods, Nick Gregory, or *any* forecaster came on, my mother made everyone in the room stop talking so she could listen—even if she'd just heard the weather report five minutes earlier. I'd learned to tune it out.

"Yeah, what about it?" I asked, lying back on the couch.

"Audrey . . ." (I really wasn't kidding about the Audrey thing.)

"Audrey said severe thunderstorms could rip through the area due to the unusually warm weather we've been having. I'm not sure you'll make it back on Friday."

Mom went on about a hot spell and a cold front, and I don't know . . . I was already zoning. Basically, she said she'd be monitoring the situation, but that if everything stayed on course, there was a good chance my flight would be canceled and I'd have to stay in Florida until Sunday.

I thanked her for the heads-up, but honestly, I didn't know why she was making such a big deal out of it. A few more days in Florida sounded nice. Bonus prize—I probably wouldn't be on the same flight back home as Zev anymore.

After I hung up, I grabbed my guitar and said good-bye to Gram. It was time to meet up with Fitz.

TEN

Zev's flowers were still sitting outside the door where he left them. I wouldn't let Gram bring them in last night. I did not need any reminders of my ex. I kicked them into the shrubs. It was time to think about my music. *What should I play for Fitz?* I debated it as I walked to meet him. I tended to go for a good love ballad when I played for someone the first time, but I didn't want to send the wrong message. Maybe something up-beat and fun instead. I wrote a song last year after having the most perfect day on Coney Island with Trina and Trevor. It was all about friendship and summer. That seemed like the best bet.

The community center where Fitz and I were set to meet was right past the pool, and it was gigantic. Anyone who lived in the retirement village was welcome to use it. The place had a ton of rooms where they held different events, and the lobby had couches and little tables set up for people to hang out. There were even a few early risers there now.

I checked out the corkboard hanging on the wall. It was filled with posters offering everything from swimming lessons and Zumba classes to card tournaments and various outings. I understood why Gram decided to move here. It was kind of like college for senior citizens without the tests and papers.

"Excuse me," I asked two women sitting down drinking coffee. "Can you point me to the gym?" That was where Fitz said he'd be all morning.

"Right down the hall and take the elevator down one flight. You won't miss it," the first one said.

"You picked a good time," the other added, leaning closer to me. "I saw a very handsome young man go down there a little while ago. On the short side, but for you it will do nicely."

I didn't know what to say. "Oh, yeah, we're just friends," I kind of sputtered out.

She raised an eyebrow. "You can change that."

"Maybe." I was getting it from everywhere. First Trina, now a stranger? Were they onto something I wasn't? *No.* I knew what was best for me, and I wasn't about to get into another discussion about my love life. Trina and I dissected it enough, so I excused myself and took the elevator down to the gym.

Fitz was the only one inside. He was lying back on the bench, a bar with an unnatural amount of weight attached to it held over his head.

"Hi," I said tentatively, not wanting to startle him. No way I was going to be responsible for that thing falling down and crushing him.

He put the weight down, and wiped some sweat off his brow with his forearm. "Hey."

I sat down on a leg-lift machine across from him. "That looked heavy."

He sat up and shrugged. "Usually do a lot more, but without a spotter I take it easy."

Easy? He and I had very different definitions of the term. Maybe he was bragging, although that didn't seem his style. He could have been looking for an offer of assistance, but I was not biting. Lifting heavy metal discs—even as backup help—was certainly not how I wanted to spend my vacation. Instead I asked him about his morning.

Fitz had been up since before seven. He said he liked to get up with the sun. We were definitely opposites. If I hadn't heard Gram yammering away on the phone at nine, I probably would have still been asleep now. "You get up that early every day?"

"Try," he said. "At school it's harder. Here it's easy to go to bed early."

I guess that depended on who you were. My gram was out late all the time. She canceled most of her usual plans because I was visiting, but from my eavesdropping (both past and present), I gathered my gram knew how to party. I must have gotten the gene from her. My parents were the ultimate homebodies—even though we lived in a city with a gazillion incredible things to do. How they didn't take advantage of it was beyond me.

"So are you going to play me something?" he asked, and jutted his chin toward my guitar.

"Here?" I'd never played in a gym before, but it was far from the worst place I'd ever played. Or even the smelliest. I sometimes went down to the subway station near my apartment. I liked singing at full blast when the trains approached. The noise masked the volume, and let me get out any pent-up emotion that I was having trouble accessing. I even wrote two of my favorite songs after my mini subway sessions.

"No one's around," he said. "Unless you have somewhere else in mind."

"This works." I took Ruby out of her case and breathed her in. Spruce, mahogany, and a twinge of something metallic. I loved that smell.

"This one is called 'Wonder of It,'" I said, and pulled Ruby closer. For this particular song I didn't use a pick. I preferred the combo of my fingers plucking the strings and my nails striking at them. It gave a soft, warm tone while also creating a rich sound.

The room was quiet. I took a breath and got started. After a few chords, I didn't need to think anymore. I just felt. I let my fingers do what they knew to do, and I began to sing, getting lost in the sounds and lyrics.

When I finished, my whole body got those little chills it always got from playing. For the first time in days, I felt like myself again. Why had I waited so long to get out my guitar? It always made me feel better. Mom would say it's because music releases dopamine, but I didn't care about the science. I cared about the feeling, and it was that surge of happiness I needed.

"Sweet," Fitz said, and put out his fist.

I had almost forgotten he was there. "Thanks," I said, with a tentative bump back.

We talked a little about my music. Like the fact that I'd been playing forever. My dad dabbled with the guitar. Apparently, he was cool at one point in time.

"Ruby was actually my father's," I said, patting my baby.

"Did you name your guitar?"

The look on his face made me laugh. "Yes, it is not that weird. At least not any weirder than people who name their cars."

He was still looking at me funny.

"I did it when I was five!" I explained. "My dad had it out in the living room one day, and I had just gotten all these rhine-stone stickers. And I, being the delightful daughter that I am, thought it would be a nice surprise to decorate his guitar for him."

"I'm sure he appreciated it," Fitz said, laughing.

I scrunched up my face. "The story goes that he turned purple when he saw my masterful artwork, but I was so excited, that he pretended he was, too, and left them on. Lucky for him, the jewel stickers were pretty cheap and fell off by the end of the week. Except for one. A ruby. So that's what I started calling the guitar. Then on my bat mitzvah, my dad gave it to me. The ruby is still there," I said, pointing to the gemstone at the base of the guitar, "and it's still holding strong today."

"All right; that explanation gets a pass," he said, smiling at me.

"I'm so glad it meets your approval," I said, and winked at him. *Winked*. What was wrong with me? *Stop flirting, Sari Silver.* You're the one who said you weren't ready for anything new. Change the subject. *Now.*

"Speaking of names," I said. "Fitz. First name, last name?" He didn't need to know that I already knew the answer, and it was a safe, platonic topic.

"It's Cameron Fitzberg, but most people call me Fitz. Even my parents say it now. They got used to hearing it from my friends, my coaches, announcers at my matches. The only ones who really use Cameron or Cam are my grandparents and my dad's side of the family."

"Cam, huh? I like that, too. A *strong* name. Fitting."

"Well, *you*, can call me whatever you want," he said, and winked back at me.

Oh my God. I was doing it again, and *he* was doing it back. Trina and Zev had teased me in the past about being a flirt, but I thought they were exaggerating. I was just friendly. I was in a relationship, I didn't think anything of it. But now I realized that they might have been right. I needed to rein it in. "If your *friends* call you Fitz," I said, "then that's what I'll call you, too." I grabbed my phone as an excuse to break eye contact.

More text messages from Zev. When was he going to clue in that I was always going to ignore them?

I also had a missed call. A non-Zev one. It was from a 212 area code.

"I'm sorry," I told Fitz. "I just need to check this message. I don't recognize the number."

"Sure."

Fitz was still his relaxed, easygoing self. If he was fazed by my on-and-off-again flirting, he didn't show it. Hopefully, he didn't even notice.

I played the message, and those little chills I had earlier turned into full-blown goose bumps. "No way, no way, NO WAY!!"

"What?" Fitz asked.

"They want me." My voice had faded to less than a whisper.

"Huh?" Fitz moved closer.

"Meta. The club. They have a spot for me *this* Saturday night."

Sheila the owner actually asked me to perform. This was unreal. I needed to call her back. ASAP. I dialed the number.

"Breathe," Fitz said, and did some sort of slow-motion arm

waving thing, but now was not the time for breathing exercises.

I turned away and focused on the call, trying not to freak out. When Sheila picked up, I wasn't sure I remembered how to talk. "Sheila," I squawked, "this is Sari Silver. I got your message."

She filled me in on the details about the performance, but she could have told me I'd have to sing standing on my head in a pit full of roaches while wearing a dress made of toilet paper and chewing gum and I would have still said yes. "Saturday sounds great. Thank you. I'll see you then."

At least that's what I think I said. After I hung up, the whole thing seemed like I conjured it in my mind. I may have pretended to have a semblance of calmness around me, but I was spinning—in the best possible way.

"I have to go," I told Fitz. I had so much to do. Pick a set list, practice, tell Gram, my mom, Trina, Ze—

Oh.

There went my euphoria. It was weird not to be able to share this with him. Trina and I did a lot of the work getting us into Meta way back when, but Zev played a big role, too. I couldn't focus on that. This was time to think about me. This was the universe making things better.

"It was so nice meeting you," I said to Fitz as I grabbed my stuff and ran out. "Have a great rest of your trip. Sorry we couldn't hang out more."

It wasn't the nicest good-bye, but I'd send him a message on GroupIt once things settled down. Right now I needed to get back to Gram's. What if Mom was right about the weather? I needed to get on an earlier flight stat. Nothing was going to screw this up for me.

I was about to live one of my biggest dreams.

New York, get ready, I'm coming home!

ELEVEN

My alarm went off, and I shot up in bed early Friday after tossing and turning all night. I was going to have to travel on a whole two hours of sleep. No matter how much I begged, my parents refused to pay the admittedly huge fee to switch me to an earlier flight. Since mine wasn't canceled, there was an exorbitant charge. All Wednesday night and all day Thursday I pleaded my case, but they held their ground.

My mother actually said, "Worst-case scenario, you'll get stuck in Florida a few days and play at Meta another time," as if the club was waiting around for me. My parents totally didn't get how important this was. To them it was no different than any of the other random gigs I did. The more I fought, the more they dug their feet in. I would have paid for it myself if I had the cash, but I'd spent everything I'd saved up on my ticket to Florida in the first place. I seriously considered using the emergency credit card they gave me to secretly book the flight, but I knew if they found out before my performance—which they would—there was no way they'd let me go do it. They'd flip. I could picture them dragging me offstage if I sneaked out. I thought Gram would come to my defense, but she just played devil's advocate. *Money was tight. College is expensive. There's just no extra funds lying around.*

I didn't want to seem ungrateful. I appreciated what they were doing for me. I knew money was an issue. My parents, Gram, and my grandparents on my dad's side were all already helping out as much as they could with the Manhattan School of Music, and I was still going to have a preposterous amount of loans by the time I graduated. It would be worth it, though. Only so was this performance. It could be my big break. I just wished they could see that.

Gram's solution was getting me to the airport way early Friday to see if I could get a standby spot. Usually, the airline didn't charge extra for that. I wanted to get there as soon as I could. The storm wasn't supposed to hit New York 'til later, so there was still hope I'd get home in time.

I jumped out of bed, tied my hair back in a quick knot, and threw on a bra underneath my NEVERTHELESS, SHE PERSISTED T-shirt. After the week I was having, it was the perfect reminder that giving up was not an option.

"Gram," I called out. "You up?"

"In the kitchen," she said.

Thank God. "Can we get going?"

"Yeah," she said. "Have some coffee, some breakfast, get dressed, and we'll get out of here."

"I'm good to go."

She looked me over, but if she had a comment on my appearance, she kept it to herself. I was still wearing the T-shirt and sweats that I had slept in, but that was by design. Some might call it wearing pajamas out of the house, but to me it was an ingenious (and comfortable) time-saver.

"Packed?" she asked.

I nodded. I had been packed since Wednesday.

"Sure I can't get you something to eat?" Gram asked.

She was always trying to feed me. But I didn't want food. I wanted to go. My current flight was scheduled for 2:00 p.m., but I really wanted to try to make the 9:00 a.m. one.

"Positive. I'll get something at the airport."

"Okay," she said. "I'm still packing you something for the road."

I didn't bother to object. If I said no, she'd only keep insisting.

She's being sweet, I reminded myself. Gram was a great host, and I had been such a lousy guest, moping most of the trip and now rushing her to drive me to the airport before she even finished her coffee. I'd make this up to her. I was going to be the perfect granddaughter. Once I got home, that is. FaceTime, phone calls, answering all her computer questions without any exasperation, devoting all my time to her on her next visit, everything. But right now, I just needed to get out of here.

I put on my sneakers, grabbed my stuff, and waited by the door. Ten minutes later we were finally in the car.

That stereotype about older drivers going, like, thirteen miles per hour on the highway? My gram definitely proved that one wrong. By the time we made it to the airport, my knuckles were white from clutching the door handle. I'd said I wanted to get there fast, but I seriously think my gram set some sort of record. If only Gram were piloting the plane.

"You have your guitar, your phone, your license, your back-pack, your suitcase, your snacks, everything?" Gram asked, running through the checklist as we stood by the passenger side of the car to say good-bye.

"I do, thank you."

"I can wait," she offered, "while you check on that earlier flight. I can take you back to my place to relax for a bit if you can't get it."

"That's okay. I should be able to get one." I crossed my fingers. There were a bunch of flights headed to New York this morning. And there was no way I was heading back to Gram's. We'd just have to turn right back around. I wasn't going to risk being late. "I have my book to keep me busy if I have to wait," I told her, and patted my backpack. I stashed the last Harry Potter book in there. Since I had my own He-Who-Must-Not-Be-Named to deal with, I figured rereading the passage about the real Voldemort being taken down would be uplifting. But I really hoped I didn't need it. I didn't want to have to wait in the airport—or see Zev. My performance was the reason I desperately wanted an early flight, but avoiding my ex was a close second.

I gave Gram a giant bear hug and she squeezed me tight. I held back tears. I hated good-byes. But I reminded myself it wasn't going to be for long. She was coming to visit over the summer.

"I love you," she said, "I know you are going to take everyone's breath away at your show. Record it for me."

"I will." I thanked her for everything and gave her one last squeeze. "I love you."

"Call me when you get home," she said, as we pulled apart.

I waved and made my way into the building.

I was finally at the airport.

TWELVE

*W*hoa. The airport was crowded. *Really* crowded. The check-in line snaked around what might as well have been miles of dividers. Either everyone had the same idea as me to try and beat the storm or it was just normal end of spring break travel— or both. Regardless, this was not looking good.

I couldn't just stand there, I had to get in line. This wait was just to get my ticket and switch my flight. Security was going to be another monstrosity altogether. I wheeled my suitcase to the back of the line. *Three* people bumped into me on the way. I mean, come on. *Watch where you're going*. It's not like they couldn't see my giant suitcase, guitar, and backpack. But I guess that extra second it would have taken to walk around me would have been too much to ask.

Okay, I needed to relax. I really should have taken Gram up on that cup of coffee. I thought being groggy at the airport wouldn't matter, that it would help me sleep on the plane. Only it was just making me irritable. All these people. And the lights. It was way too bright in here. This sucked. I glanced at my phone: 8:20. At this rate, no way I was going to catch the 9:00 a.m. flight, I'd be lucky to make my original one.

Stop it, Sari. Positive thinking. I had great airport karma. My flight down here was awesome. The way home would be, too. The line was going to move, I'd get home, have the night to relax, and have a killer performance tomorrow. I just needed to distract myself. I ran through my track list for my set. I spent all day yesterday working on it. Sheila was giving me a fifty-minute set, so I had time for twelve songs. I was going to do a combo of originals and covers, with a variety of tempos. It took me forever to choose, but I was confident in my final selection.

I was going to start slow. A Kevin Wayward ballad that would really show off my vocals. Then I'd switch to something upbeat. The one I played for Fitz the other day. I ran the two songs in my head.

Usually, singing to myself calmed me. Right now it was making me anxious. *Two whole songs*, and I hadn't budged in line. I needed to get home.

I checked the time again.

8:29. The 9:00 a.m. flight wasn't going to happen. But there was a 10:00 a.m. I could still make that.

8:38. I moved forward ten feet. *Ten?!* I *really* should have had that coffee.

8:43. No additional movement.

8:46. Still nothing. *Seriously?* I stood on my tippy toes to try and see what the holdup was. How hard was it to show your ID, put your bag on the scale, collect your ticket, and get out of the way? You didn't need to stand there asking a gazillion questions.

8:55. I advanced another six feet. Total. *That's it.* It didn't help that a family of five rushed in claiming they were about to miss their flight and got moved to the front of the line. I was tempted to try the same thing, but I thought better of it. The flight I *wanted* to take was leaving soon, my *actual* flight wasn't leaving for hours. I didn't think my fellow passengers would appreciate the nuance.

"I can't believe it's this slow today," I said half to myself, half to the woman behind me. "It wasn't like this when I left New York."

"Everyone's trying to get out before the storm hits," she answered.

"It's not supposed to hit 'til later," I said. In the past thirty-six hours, I'd become more obsessed with the weather than my mother.

The woman sneered. "This is the *airport*. My flight got delayed eight hours on the way here on Tuesday. And that was gorgeous weather. Today's going to be a mess."

She was making it very hard to stay optimistic.

The woman pulled the handle up on her suitcase and headed out of line. "The kiosks look faster. I'm going there."

"Wait," I said. "You can do it there even if you have to check your baggage?"

She nodded.

I wasn't sure what to do.

The line I was in wasn't getting me anywhere, but if I left, I'd still have to get through security before I could try for standby at the actual gate. Which was faster? I looked over at the kiosks, the woman was already at one. I hadn't budged since she left. Maybe she had the right idea. Even if I made it to the front of this line, got a standby flight, there'd be no guarantee I'd get through security in time to actually catch it. That did it. I knew what I had to do.

I took a deep breath and got out of line. I prayed the airport gods were with me.

So far, the kiosk seemed like the right move. I finished in minutes. I regretted not heading there straight from the get-go. I shook off the thought. No time for regrets—just moving forward. I dumped my suitcase on the conveyer belt. It was nice to have one less thing to carry. I made my way to security and you guessed it—another endless line. It was like I was in a production of *Waiting for Godot*.

I shifted my backpack on my shoulder and moved my guitar case to the other hand. I was in this new line for less than a minute and I was already antsy. Trina would have recommended being productive right now. She'd be getting homework, reading, *something* done. I couldn't focus. All I could think about was how bad I needed to get home.

I felt boxed in, like the room was closing in around me. I was not typically a claustrophobic person, I loved a huge crowd at a concert, but this line was turning me into one. There was a couple in front of me kissing every three seconds. And a guy behind me who didn't seem to understand the meaning of personal space. It was like he thought that extra centimeter between us would somehow be the difference between getting on his flight or not. Every time I tried to inch away, he just inched forward. The turns and nasty glares I threw back at him didn't seem to have any effect.

"Do you mind?" I finally said, when he brushed into my backpack for the thirteenth time.

"Sorry," he said, like he hadn't even noticed me there.

Maybe he hadn't. I was just on edge. And the two people practically groping each other in front of me weren't helping.

PDA was the worst. I probably would have thought they were sweet a week ago, but now I felt the urge to pull the guy's hand out of the woman's back pocket. Was this how annoying Zev and I used to look? I was so done with public displays of affection. People needed to just keep to themselves and think about the others around them. Others who could very well be suffering from a broken heart.

I grabbed the bag that Gram gave me. Maybe there were some decent snacks in there. Something to take my mind off *love*. Well, the romantic kind anyway.

There was a little container of her famous peanut butter cookies. I shoved them back in the bag. They were another reminder of Zev. He had been talking about them nonstop since I saved him a few after Gram baked some on Thanksgiving. No one made them like she did. I'd even asked her to make them special for this trip. I didn't have the heart to tell her I was no longer in the mood. Instead, I just avoided the cookie jar.

There was also an apple, a string cheese, and a yogurt. Nothing spoke to me. I considered the yogurt as I inched forward in line. I liked the flavor—strawberry—but I really just wanted caffeine. Coffee, chocolate, Red Bull. Something to wake me up.

"Ya know, they won't let you through security with that," someone said.

I looked up. "Fitz!"

This time no fist bump. Just a head nod. His hands were too full. He had a duffel bag in one and what looked like a scrambled-egg wrap in the other. "I can't believe I'm running into you here," I said, "I thought you were leaving yesterday."

"Nope, today."

When we had been chatting by the pool he told me he was heading back in a couple of days—which technically meant two days—so it wasn't my fault I assumed he was talking about Thursday. I still felt bad, though. His grandpa didn't drive, which meant he'd had to pay for a car.

"I'm sorry; I would have given you a ride."

"No worries. I got stuff done on the way here and had enough time to grab some food."

"You were smart. I'm not in the mood for this," I said, pointing to the yogurt.

"You should eat it now. They count it as a liquid, and it's over the limit."

Figured. "Want it?" I asked.

"If you're not gonna have it, sure."

I handed him the spoon, too. And then he went on about how if I liked strawberries, I should check out the smoothie place just past security, that it was one of the best.

I was more of Frappuccino girl myself. I preferred to eat my fruit, not drink it. But since the line started moving again, separating me and Fitz, I just said, "Sounds good."

Keeping my eye out for Fitz as we made our way through the line kind of became a game for me—at the very least a distraction. He was about twenty or so people ahead of me, which meant when I was about halfway down my row, we wound up next to each other again, separated only by a thin piece of fabric divider. Talking to him in those brief encounters broke up the monotony of waiting.

We had flights on the same airline. His was at 11:00 a.m. I was still shooting for the 10:00 a.m., but since boarding was at

9:30, I'd need to get out of this line and to an agent really quickly to make that happen.

We continued through the maze, and eventually Fitz got to the front of the line and handed over his passport.

A little while later it was my turn. Then it was off to the final stretch. I slipped off my sneakers and waited until I was close enough to toss them in a bin along with my bag of liquids. I propped my backpack and guitar on the table. It was nine thirty-two. Maybe if I raced through this and to the gate, I'd still get a seat on the next flight.

"Push your stuff forward and step up," the agent said.

I went into the X-ray machine, put my hands above my head, and waited as the contraption did its thing. I glanced at the monitor by the agent and let out a light groan. Two sections were lit up. Apparently, there was something suspect on my arm and chest.

"Please step over here," the agent said. "Have a seat, it will just be a minute," he told me, and then called out, "Need a pat down."

Just perfect. I could forget the 10:00 a.m.

"Can I at least get my stuff?" I asked. I hated that Ruby, my phone, wallet, etc., were just sitting there unattended.

"It'll be fine," he said.

I looked for Fitz, hoping he'd grab my things for me, but he was gone. I kind of thought he would wait, since his flight was later than mine, but I guess not. I was a little disappointed.

The female agent came by five minutes later. Yeah, the 10:00 a.m. was definitely out.

"I don't know why my arm lit up," I said, lifting my sleeve.

"There's nothing there. And the other is probably my bra. There's an underwire."

"Arms out," was all she said.

She was just doing her job, I knew that, but I still couldn't help but cringe as she did the pat down. I could not catch a break today.

When I finally got the clear, I went to grab my things. I sat by a nearby bench and put on my sneakers.

"Surprise." I looked up.

It was Fitz, holding a smoothie. "I thought you could use this," he said.

"Thank you." That was so sweet of him. I forced myself to take a sip and smile. The gesture was so nice, I wasn't going to refuse the drink, even though I wasn't in the mood for it. "Really, this was totally sweet." The 10:00 a.m. flight was out, but the 11:00 a.m. was looking better and better.

Fitz and I headed to the terminal together. I stumbled getting onto the moving walkway. Fortunately, I caught myself before I sent smoothie everywhere.

"Careful," he said.

"I'm not a klutz, I promise." I wasn't. It was just the cup was wet and slippery and getting on and off those walkways tended to trip me up. Same with escalators. I always took one beat too long before making my move. I'd heard too many horror stories about shoelaces getting caught and people falling. It was another downside of my mom watching so much weather, the news was always left on, and I heard a lot of stories I could have lived without.

"No judgments," he said. Then he told me a story about how he added a pull-up bar to his dorm-room door, but didn't install it right, and fell on his butt just as his roommate and friends walked in.

We laughed and told embarrassing stories the rest of the way to the terminal. Maybe things weren't so bad, after all.

Or maybe they were.

Right as we neared the end of the moving walkway, I saw a familiar figure looming by the first gate in the terminal.

Zev.

Not again. Why was he here? It was way too early. He wasn't supposed to be at the airport for hours.

He caught my eye, and everything that could go wrong did.

I was so focused on him, that I didn't realize I had made it to the end of the walkway. I lost my footing and lunged forward. I caught myself. Sort of. *I* didn't fall. But my smoothie did. Cold, bright-pink liquefied fruit was all over my feet, my sweats, and the floor.

Yep. That good airport karma I used to have?

It was long, long gone.

THIRTEEN

Fitz went to get napkins to help clean up my mess, which just left me and Zev. Sure, there were people moving all around us, but they just blurred in the background. All I could see was my ex. He was five feet away and taking a step forward.

"Do not come any closer," I warned him. "Just go.".

"Sari, please let's just talk."

"What's there to talk about, Zev? I walked in on you kissing your ex. Seems pretty cut and dried to me." All the memories from that night washed over me, and I gripped the guitar case handle. "I can't do this right now. You want to do something for me? Stay here, make sure no one slips, and clean this thing up when Fitz gets back. I'm going to go change."

"Who's Fitz—" I heard him start to say.

I didn't answer. I just took off my shoes and ran to the nearest restroom. Fortunately, it wasn't too crowded. I dropped my stuff in the corner and looked in the mirror.

You are not going to cry. You are capable, confident, and can do whatever you set your mind to. I didn't feel very confident, though. I felt like a mess. I looked like one, too. *Time to change that.* My sneakers weren't salvageable. They were white tennis shoes. At least they used to be. Now they were sticky, wet pink ones. I was never getting that out of the nylon. I tossed them in the trash, fished through my backpack, and found what I was looking for. I had stashed away my favorite black maxidress and a pair of sky-high heels. It wasn't my first choice for airport attire, but maybe it was just what I needed. Just because I felt like crap, didn't mean I had to look like it. I changed out of the dirty sweats and T-shirt and into the dress. My new outfit was already picking up my mood. I decided to take it one step further.

I put my makeup bag and phone on the counter. There wasn't anyone too nearby, so I punched up Trina's name and FaceTimed her. I hoped it wasn't too creepy, doing that in a bathroom, but I really needed to talk to her *and* have both of my hands free to do my makeup.

"Hello," she yawned.

"Did I wake you?" She was always up early, I was the one who usually slept the morning away.

"Yeah, I didn't get home 'til really late last night," she said, rubbing her face.

"What happened to the curfew?" I asked.

Trina's eyes lit up. "There was none. Keisha went back to her dorm and took me with her. My first college party."

"Wait. You and your sister actually hung out?! At a party? I thought you were ready to kill her," I said, pulling out my mascara and getting to work.

"I was. All the know-it-all stuff she'd been spewing, but she totally made up for it. This party seriously put all of our high school ones to shame." She bit her lip, probably realizing just about anything would be better than the last party we'd been to together. She quickly got off that point. "Next year, you are totally coming to all of the NYU parties with me."

I loved that we were both going to college in the city. "Definitely."

Trina leaned in, her face becoming bigger on my screen. "Why are you putting on enough contour to rival a Kardashian?"

"Because," I said, using my fingers to blend the shadows, "we can't all wake up looking like a beauty queen like you."

"Oh, please," she said.

But it was true. Trina was naturally beautiful.

"Like you're one to talk. You know you're pretty," she added. "Besides you barely wear makeup at school, why are you doing this for the airport?"

"If I have to be stuck with Voldemort, I might as well make him see what he's missing."

"Wait, he's there?!"

I nodded.

"How could you let me go on about my sister, when you had a run-in with *him*?"

"Believe me, the distraction was welcome." I ran my fingers through my hair, trying to detangle the curls.

"Did you talk?" she asked.

I told her what happened with Fitz being there and the smoothie.

"This is actually amazing," she said, sitting up in her bed. "Zev is going to flip over seeing you with Fitz. He'll be so jealous. If you haven't made a move yet, now is the time."

"Trina."

"I'm serious."

"Yeah," I said, "I know you are." I let out a sigh. "It's just seeing Zev. I still want him."

"You're not taking him back, are you?"

"What? No! There's no way. Not after what he did. Just seeing him was hard, though. I need more time to get over it."

"I'm sorry."

"I'll be fine," I said as I slipped on the heels and moved the phone so she could get a clear look at the final results.

"Amazing," she said. "Zev is not going to know what to do with himself."

"Thanks." I actually felt good. I had shoved the dress and shoes into my bag as a safety, in case my luggage got lost. I was going to wear them for my performance, and I wasn't risking an airport screwup and them winding up in South Dakota or Hawaii. Luckily, my over-preparedness was coming in handy today.

Trina and I said our good-byes, and I headed back into the main concourse, with my head held high.

Zev Geller could eat his heart out.

FOURTEEN

itz and Zev were still standing where I had left them, only they were talking and smiling. *Seriously?* I guess I shouldn't have been surprised. Fitz was so laid-back and chill. And *everybody* liked Zev. Well, everybody but me. He was one of those guys who managed to transcend the high school hierarchy. He was easygoing and funny and every group seemed to welcome him. They all smiled at him in the halls and said hello. It wasn't like we were a particularly unfriendly school or anything, but for the most part, if you weren't friends with someone, you just kind of ignored them in the halls and went on with your day. But not Zev. He was a regular Mr. Rogers, well, if Mr. Rogers had been a little more hipster looking, snarky, and a cheater.

Both guys seemed to notice me walking toward them at the same time. It may have been my imagination or wishful thinking, but I'm pretty sure both of their jaws dropped slightly.

"Thought I'd slip into something a little less comfortable," I said. "And a little cleaner."

"You look, I mean, you . . . ," Zev stumbled.

I ignored him. "Thanks for cleaning up the mess," I said to

Fitz. "Sorry I bolted. I just needed to get those shoes off." Although I was beginning to feel the same about my current ones. They had four-inch heels and were already starting to irritate me.

"Your friend did most of it," Fitz said.

"I'm her—"

"Classmate," I finished Zev's sentence, before he could say *boyfriend*. Because *that* he definitely wasn't.

Fitz seemed to sense something was up, but he didn't comment. "Should we get to the gate?" he asked instead.

Oh. My. God. Here I was worrying about my outfit and Zev, when I should have been focusing on getting an earlier flight home. How had I let him distract me like this? Getting the ticket should have been the first thing I'd done. Zev was ruining everything again. "Yes," I said, "I need that earlier flight."

I followed Fitz to gate 7. And Zev followed me. I didn't say anything. I just concentrated on my steps. The heels were pinching at my toes and burning the soles of my feet, and I'd only walked half a terminal in them. The shoes were for the look, not actually for getting around. Especially on hard, cold floors. It was as if each step reverberated inside my body. And lugging a bulky backpack and guitar wasn't making it any easier. *The pain is in your mind.* At least that was what I was trying to convince myself because I needed to keep moving.

At the gate, Fitz told me, and unfortunately Zev, that he'd get us some seats. I got in yet another line to see the ticket agent. This time there were only two people ahead of me. And once again an annoying passenger right at my back.

"Stop following me," I told Zev.

"I'm not. I just want an earlier flight, too."

Yeah, right. I shook my head and took out my book. We both knew he was only at the airport right now because he thought I was going to try and catch an earlier flight like I did on the way down here.

"Sari—"

"Reading," I said.

"I just want to—"

"What part of 'reading' don't you understand?"

"You and that guy . . . ," his voice trailed off.

"No business of yours," I said, refusing to look up from *Harry Potter and the Deathly Hallows*. "You saw to that."

"Please just tell me you and the Incredible Hulk are not together."

"I like to think of him more as Captain America." This time I peered over the pages to sneer at him.

He must have realized he wasn't getting anywhere, so he switched tactics. "He mentioned something about you having a performance to get back to. What's that about?"

This one stung. Zev had always been so confident that I'd get to perform at Meta. He even helped Trina and me convince the owner to let us in. He was the one who bought the fluorescent wristbands the club uses for the under-twenty-one crowd. He left them there with a note about how important getting in was to us and how we'd promise to wear them. Sheila finally gave in. But she made us swear we wouldn't spread the word—she didn't want her club filled with eighteen-year-olds. Not calling Zev to tell him about my performance had been really hard.

"Meta. Tomorrow night," I said quietly.

"Sari, that's amazing. This is huge. Congratulations. I knew you'd get in there sooner or later." He looked so happy for me that I felt my eyes well up. "Which songs are you doing?" he asked. "Are you going to end with 'Living, Loving, You'?" That was the song I wrote about him. It was my best, but I didn't have it on my list. I didn't think I could get through it.

I shook my head.

He kept peppering me with questions, but fortunately the agent called me up.

I pushed Zev and my burning feet out of my mind and flashed the woman my biggest smile. "Hi, I was hoping you could please help me. I'm supposed to be on the two p.m. back to New York, but I was wondering if there was room on any of the earlier ones. I know there's an 11:01, a 12:22. I don't care if it takes me into LaGuardia, JFK, Newark; any of them is fine."

"Me too," Zev said joining me. "We're together."

I was going to kill him, but I didn't want to make a scene. I wanted help, not to be dragged away by the TSA for strangling my ex-boyfriend. "My seat is the priority," I told the woman. "If you can just get one, that's fine."

She said she'd take a look, and I thanked her profusely. Only it didn't matter how much I groveled. They were all booked solid. "I could put you on standby for the 11:01. You'd be numbers three and four."

"That would be amazing, yes, thank you," I said.

I was feeling slightly hopeful. There was a storm brewing back home, so there was a chance a bunch of people would decide to stick it out in Florida for a few days. I just needed a family of three to cancel, and I'd be all set. Otherwise I could still use my original ticket for 2:00 p.m. So far, there hadn't been any flights canceled. I just needed that to last a little longer.

After we finished at the counter, Zev continued to follow me.

"Enough," I said.

"I just need you to hear me out," he said. "What happened at the party. It's not what it looked like."

"No?" I said, straining to keep my volume low. "Did Bethanne put an evil spell on you that magically caused you to kiss? Maybe your lips just fell onto hers? I don't need pathetic excuses, Zev. I don't want to hear it."

He put his hand on my arm. "Sari . . ."

I yanked it away. "Do not touch me."

"I'm sorry."

"Go." I took a step back.

"I will," Zev said, "just please, hear me out first."

"I told you before, there's nothing to hear."

"Sari, you need to listen to what I have to say."

I don't know what came over me, if it was the way he said my name, or the memories he was bringing up, but somehow—and I don't even remember doing it—I chucked my copy of *Harry Potter and the Deathly Hallows* right at him as I said, "I told you to go."

Only he jumped out of the way and the book whacked the guy sitting about five feet away from us in the back.

My hand flew over my mouth. Oh my God. What did I do?

I just threw a book at a stranger. I was not a violent person. Yet here I was flinging one of my favorite stories of all time at a random guy. On the upside, my throw was kind of weak and it was the paperback, not the hardcover, but still . . . it was massive.

The guy turned around. He did not look happy. Not that I blamed him. Someone, namely me, had just thrown *Harry Potter* at his back.

"What the hell was that?" he growled.

I was so getting kicked out of the airport. "I'm sor—"

Zev cut me off. "It was me," he said. "I'm really sorry. We've been stuck here, feeling cooped up, and I was joking around. Pretending to save her from one of the seven Horcruxes. But I aimed a little too far with my throw."

The guy looked confused. "Hor-what?"

WHAT WAS HE DOING?

"You know in Harry Potter," Zev explained, "the objects where dark wizards hide parts of their soul like in Tom Riddle's diary. Sorry that was a spoiler. Please tell me you've already read the series."

"No," the guy said.

"Okay, you need to read it," Zev told him. "I don't care how old you are, this book is worth your time."

Only Zev would spin a story like that and wind up giving out a book recommendation while simultaneously taking the fall for me. He was such a dork. It was part of the reason I'd fallen for him.

Here he was turning the man I basically assaulted into his new best friend. Seriously, he was standing there offering to buy the guy book one to make up for everything. They were laughing and somehow the conversation turned to stupid stunts they had each pulled off in public.

Mr. Popularity struck again. The guy had a gift.

Zev made his way back to me, the book lying on top of his

open palms. He gave a slight bow and grinned at me. "Your tome, my lady."

I hated that he was being cute and helpful. I hated that when he smiled that little dimple made me want to smile back. I hated that after everything he had done, I still missed him. A lot. I grabbed the book from his hands. "Thank you," I said, quickly shoving it in my backpack. I was not going to let my willpower falter. Charming did not equal trustworthy, and that's what I wanted.

"Now can we talk?" he asked.

"Just because you helped me, doesn't mean you get something in return."

"I know," he said.

"Good." I headed toward Fitz, who was seated near the wall. I could still feel Zev behind me, his shadow looming. I turned around to face him. "How many times do I have to tell you, there's nothing to say?"

He picked at his thumbnail. He always did that when he was nervous. "*I* have something to say."

"I don't care. I want you out of my life, Zev."

"You'll throw away a whole year, everything we have, without even talking?"

I shrugged my shoulder. I wasn't the one who trashed what we had—the blame for that was solely on him.

"No," he said, shaking his head. "I'm not going to let you do that. You were the one who showed me that if something's important to you, you don't give up. You're performing at Meta tomorrow. You fought for that. You would have done almost anything for a shot. That's how I feel about you. I'm going to prove it to you. You'll see."

"Don't waste your time," I told him.

"I'm not," he said. "Fighting for what you want is never a waste."

I just turned on my heels and walked away from him, before I said something I'd totally regret. . . .

FIFTEEN

Fitz moved his bag off one of the empty seats next to him when he saw me, and I sat down.

"Get the flight?" he asked, pulling his headphones away from his ears.

I held up my crossed fingers. "On standby."

He nodded.

I wasn't really in the mood to talk, so I took out my headphones, too, and put them on. I glanced around for signs of Zev. He hadn't followed me and was nowhere to be seen. My words must have gotten through to him. That was a good thing, I reminded myself.

I put my music list on shuffle, and within seconds of closing my eyes, I felt my seat shift. Someone took the chair next to me, and I didn't need to look to know who it was. So much for getting through. . . .

"An espresso Frappuccino with two percent," Zev said.

My go-to stress drink. Zev knew that. I wanted it so bad. I could say no, and then go buy my own, but then Fitz would probably wonder why. I didn't want to explain my drama.

I peeked over at him. "No, thanks."

"Come on," he said, and dangled the drink. "I had them hold the whipped cream." I hated whipped cream. To me it tasted like watered-down ice cream.

"Not thirsty." Although my mouth was starting to salivate.

"If you don't take it, you know I'm just going to throw it away." Zev didn't do coffee, he didn't like the flavor. He wouldn't even touch tiramisu or coffee ice cream. I should have known something was wrong with him right there.

"Fine," I said, "but only because I think it would be a waste. It doesn't change things."

"I know," he said, but was smiling all the same. I took the drink and looked away. I didn't want to see that dimple.

"Tell me more about the performance," he said.

I swirled the straw around in my drink. I really shouldn't be talking to him. "It's at eight," I said. Ugh. Why did I do that? He was bound to show up now. A part of me wanted that, but not the smart part.

I took out my phone and texted Trina.

> 911. Zev is here. Caving.
> So messed up. Help.

My phone instantly started to ring. I left my stuff and took the call over by the window. "Sari, you know I support you a hundred percent . . . ," Trina said. I stared out at the planes on the tarmac. This sounded like the start to something I didn't want to hear. "If you want to get back together with him, I have your back. But . . . ," she paused.

"What? What is it?"

"It's Bethanne." I could hear the hesitation in her voice.

"She's been posting on GroupIt again. I didn't want to say anything, but you should see what she's writing underneath the pictures of her and Zev before you even consider letting him back in."

I told her I'd call her back later and immediately punched up GroupIt. I had already seen the picture of Zev with his arm around Bethanne, but it still made me cringe. Only now there were a bunch of comments below it.

"You can't keep a dynamic duo apart," Bethanne wrote. It got a bunch of likes. Someone responded, "his girlfriend may object." She answered with, "what girlfriend? ;) Mr. Geller is a free man, he told me himself. But this was just a one-night-only reunion special. Who wants a boyfriend senior year?"

I felt a knot in my throat, like a Ping-Pong ball was stuck in there. There it was for the whole world to see. Here I was, a teeny, tiny part of me actually thinking maybe, possibly I could fix things with Zev, that I should hear him out like he'd been begging me to do, but it would have all been for nothing—it wasn't me he wanted.

Other than today and when he showed up at my gram's door, the only communication I'd had with him was super late last Friday night when I texted him that we were over. The only people who knew we broke up were my family, Trina, and Zev himself. Trina said she wasn't going to say anything.

But somehow Bethanne knew.

Zev told her.

He must have gotten in touch with her to say he was single. But since she apparently didn't want him, instead preferring to be single senior year, here he was crawling back to me.

I was a fool. How could I buy into the whole "you're worth

fighting for, I love you" nonsense? Zev was amazing at improv, of course he could lay it on thick. Just look what he did with the Harry Potter book guy. And I fell for it.

I glared in his direction. He was looking right at me. I walked to the trash can and in the most exaggerated fashion possible, dropped the drink in, and made my way back to my seat.

"You're such an ass," I hissed at him, quiet enough so Fitz wouldn't hear over his headphones.

"What? What did I do?" Zev asked.

I just rolled my eyes. Then I moved closer to Fitz, and tapped his arm.

It was Zev's turn to know what it felt like to be second choice.

SIXTEEN

"**W**hatcha listening to?" I asked Fitz.

It was the sound of the ocean. He said it helped him relax. I wanted to say there were hundreds of thousands of amazing calming songs that would be so much better than just waves, but I bit my tongue. This conversation was for Zev's benefit, not Fitz's. So instead, I told him I'd need to download the track and complimented his choice.

If Zev thought I was a flirt in the past, he'd seen nothing yet. For the next ten minutes, I listened intently to everything Fitz had to say, laughed at jokes that weren't funny, and playfully touched his arm. Zev tried to get in on the conversation, but I edged him out. I positioned my back toward him and made myself a partition between him and Fitz. Bethanne wasn't the only girl who didn't want Zev anymore.

The woman at the counter said something over the speaker but it was hard to hear. She sounded like the teacher from Charlie Brown.

"What did she say?" I asked.

"I don't know," a guy across from me said.

I stood up and headed toward the gate. I wasn't alone. A

crowd had gathered there. "I'm sorry," the agent said. "The flight has been canceled."

It seemed everyone started talking at once, firing questions and complaints at her.

"How come?" "Can I get on the next flight?" "I need to get home." "Are the rest of the flights still running?" The last one was me. I didn't get an answer.

Fitz checked his phone, he had an email and text from the airline. "They put me on the eight p.m. There's no way that's getting out of here tonight. I'm going to go see if I can get an earlier flight. Maybe I can get on yours."

If mine was still running.

I went toward gate 1, where the 2:00 p.m. would be taking off from. It was on the opposite side of the airport. I made it about halfway before I had to stop and take off my shoes. Was it too late to go fish through the trash for my sneakers? They might have been wet and sticky, but at least that was better than walking on what felt like burning stakes.

"I have a pair of socks if you want them," Zev said.

"The only thing I want from you is to leave me alone."

He shook his head. "Sari, what did I do? I thought things were starting to get a little better between us. What happened?"

"Ask Bethanne."

He stood there waiting for me to say more, but I didn't. I focused on my bag. I had my own socks in there somewhere. Not that I could find them. *Great. Just great.* I guess I was going barefoot, because I wasn't going to stand there waiting for Zev to interrogate me some more. Although the way my trip was going, I was probably going to wind up with a foot fungus.

"You don't need to come with me," I hissed at him.

"We're going to the same place," he said, his voice quiet.

I didn't need the reminder.

I breathed a small sigh of relief when I reached my gate. The board above said the flight was still on time. It really needed to stay that way.

Unfortunately, all I could do now was wait.

"You'll get home in time for the concert," Zev said, reading my mind like he always did. It was a lot more endearing when I liked him. Now it was just annoying.

"You don't know that."

"We'll make this work," he said. "You'll see."

"*We* won't do anything." I needed to get away from him. One more second of listening to Zev trying to play the knight in shining armor was bound to make me explode. I just needed to sit and relax.

Not too far from me there was an empty row, but that meant Zev would plop down next to me. There was also a solo space next to a mom and her three kids—one of whom was running in circles pretending to be an airplane, the second crying on the woman's lap, and the third bouncing in her seat like it was a trampoline. The choice was clear—the mom and the kids. I'd take three screaming children under the age of five over Zev in a heartbeat.

After about ten minutes, though, I was thinking maybe I should have found a third option.

"Jennifer, leave the girl's hair alone," the mother instructed her daughter. She had been tugging at my hair and wrapping it around her fingers.

"It's okay," I said, as the mom tried to pry the strands from her daughter's tight fist with one hand while holding onto her baby with the other.

"Sorry," she said. "Jennifer, let go."

"It's okay. Honestly, this has been the least stressful part of my day so far."

"That good, huh?" she asked, finally freeing my hair. She put a cartoon on her phone and handed it to the little girl. Within seconds the child was zombified in front of the screen, and it was like I didn't exist. If only that would work with Zev.

"Yep," I said, glancing over at my ex. He was diagonally across from me, watching everything I did. "So," I said changing the subject. "Heading home or are you Florida based?"

"Hopefully heading home." She looked up at the departure board. "But the weather has me worried."

"Me too. Are you flying to New York, too?"

She shook her head. "Connecticut, but my husband says they've already started canceling flights there. I've already been delayed two hours." I did not want to hear that. The storm was supposed to head north, if Connecticut was already having issues, the city was probably a disaster. "Everything is so disorganized here," she continued, "they changed my gate but I didn't find out until most of the seats by the new flight were taken. I'm not moving again until I know what's going on for sure. I'm afraid we might not make it home tonight."

"Home, home, home," the little kid circling in front of us started chanting loudly. "I want to go home, I want to go home, I want to go home."

The woman tried to console him. "I know, baby. Why don't you watch the show with your sister?"

"No, I want to go home," he cried.

"If you can avoid traveling solo with three kids. Do it," his mother told me.

But I knew exactly how the kid felt. I wanted to scream about going home, too. If I didn't think I'd get kicked out, or become a viral video, I might have joined him.

"I hope they call us soon," she said, looking at the departures again. "Did you say you were on this New York flight?"

"Yeah, why?" I asked.

She pointed to the board.

It had changed. And not for the better.

My flight was canceled.

SEVENTEEN

No. No. No. NO. Why was this happening to me? What had I done to deserve this? I took back what I said last week about flying. It sucked. I absolutely hated the airport.

I checked my email. "This makes no sense," I mumbled to myself.

"Michigan?" Zev asked, wheeling his carry-on toward me.

I nodded. I couldn't believe they were trying to route me there. There was no logic to it.

"Me too," he said.

I was too upset to even tell him to get lost. Right now it was the airline that had all my fury. Instead of my direct flight to New York, they rebooked me on one to Michigan in two hours that would then connect to the city. It was so stupid. I didn't need to go farther north, let alone west, to come back down and over.

I stood up and moved closer to the main departure board. Zev followed. "We're just going to wind up stuck there," I said. "They've already canceled a bunch of flights. If I'm going to get stuck somewhere, I'd rather it be Florida." Not that I wanted to be stuck anywhere. I had to get home. "Wait," I said, studying the board, "the 12:22 and the 3:15 p.m. are still running. Why is our flight canceled?"

"No idea," Zev said. He nodded toward the agents ahead. "It doesn't look like they know, either."

It was true. They looked overwhelmed. One wasn't even dealing with passengers, she was just going through some printed sheets. The other was staring silently at his computer screen while a man stood there waiting. A huge line had already formed.

I needed to get in it, too, so I could get rebooked. I turned to go and smashed my toe into Zev's suitcase.

"Damn it, Zev," I moaned. Even the simplest things were tripping me up. I guess that happened when you were focused on salvaging the remnants of what used to be your life.

"What?"

"You and your stupid bag. You're always in my way. Why are you even standing here? Why aren't you in one of those other lines?" I knew it wasn't his fault. I was the one who was barefoot. I was the one who ran into his carry-on. Even though he was the one to bring that ridiculous thing. It was like titanium or something. He had been so impressed by how sturdy it was when he got it. The dumbest things made him happy.

"Okay, I'm going." He held up his hands. "I'll take the line there," he pointed to the one a couple of gates away. "You take the one here. We'll see who gets to the front first. I'll text you if I manage to get an earlier flight, so that you can get on it, too, okay?"

"Yeah, whatever," I said, and moved to the line closest to us. At this point, I would have made a deal with the devil if it got me home.

"Sari!"

"What?" I snapped.

"Are you okay?"

It was Fitz.

"Sorry," I said, rubbing the back of my neck. "Thought you were someone else. I'm just fed up."

"Yeah," he commiserated, taking the spot behind me. His luck was about as bad as mine. He had actually gotten standby on my flight, three minutes before it was canceled.

"Unbelievable," I said. "This place is a mess."

"Tell me about it. Look at that," he said, nodding his head toward a woman cutting the front of the line and going directly to the agent. "I don't get people sometimes."

No way. This was not happening. Not today. Not on my watch. "Excuse me," I called out. "There's a line."

"I just have a quick question," she said, waving me off, like I was the one being rude and unreasonable.

Uh-uh. I was not having it. I'd been in too many lines today to let some random woman mosey on up and make the rest of us wait even longer. "Lots of people here just have a quick question. That's why there's a line. One you need to get in."

"Mind your own business," she said.

"*Excuse me*? Your cutting in front of me *is* my business." Was I seriously getting in a fight with a stranger in the airport? "You need to move." Apparently, I was. That's how pissed I had become.

"It will just take two seconds," she said, and started showing her ticket to the agent.

"I don't care." It was like my mouth had a mind of its own. And that mind had very strong beliefs on what was right and what was wrong—and self-entitlement belonged in the wrong category. Not that I was much better causing a scene and all. Still . . . I was not risking her taking the seat I needed to get home. "You're not going to let her cut in front of everyone, are you?" I asked the agent. "There's a whole line that's been waiting."

Fitz and everyone else around us were silent. Probably waiting to see what I'd do if the agent let the shrew have her way.

The agent hemmed for a moment. The lady kept shoving her ticket in his face, but I kept my eyes laser focused on him. I wasn't letting him off the hook. He had to do what was right. I needed this.

"Sorry, ma'am," he told her. "You do have to get in line."

"This is ridiculous," she said, and stormed off, whipping her hair behind her as she stalked away. "Hope you miss your flight," she muttered to me as she passed.

"Likewise," I shot back. But I didn't care, she could scowl and hate me as much as she wanted. I finally had a win today. It was small, and likely wouldn't change anything, but it made me feel like some things in the universe were right and just.

"Thank you," the guy in front of me said.

"Yeah," Fitz said, "I for one am impressed. Remind me not to get on your bad side."

"I may have overreacted."

"No, you were in the right," he said.

I smiled. I felt like I could breathe a little easier, like a tiny bit of my anger disappeared along with her. Although with my current luck, this woman would come back to haunt me in the future. "You know she's going to wind up being one of my professors next year."

Fitz laughed. "Or a major recording scout."

"My dad's boss," I suggested.

"Or maybe," Fitz said, "she's just an overentitled, selfish woman whom you'll never have to deal with again; who finally got what she deserved."

"I like that option best," I said. "Although too bad it didn't do anything. This line is still at a crawl."

"Maybe one of those phone stations would be faster," he said. There was one not too far from us. They were basically a cluster of phones that dialed straight to an airline rep. Ideally one that could help right away. But there was also a chance the person would leave you on hold for an eternity. At least here, you got to see how far off you were and look the agent in the eye.

"I'm going to stick it out here," I said.

"How about this?" Fitz offered. "I'll try the phone, you wait and see what happens here, and then we compare notes."

"Sounds like a plan," I said. I looked around the terminal. I saw Zev standing in a line similar to mine. He was about six people from the front—not any better than me. I accidentally caught his eye but looked away as he waved.

The minutes dragged on. Fitz was still by the phones. He had it to his ear, but he wasn't speaking. He was probably listening to hold music. Half an hour later, I finally made it to the agent.

"What about the twelve o'clock flight?" I asked.

"Booked and leaving soon."

"The three p.m.?"

"Also booked," he said.

"How about standby?" I pleaded.

"There's too many in front of you; you won't make it."

I was so frustrated. Flights before and after me were still taking off, but mine was canceled. There was no pilot. The one flying to Florida and then back to New York didn't make it in due to the weather. I took a deep breath. "Isn't there anything I can do?"

"You can keep the flight to Michigan, and hope it leaves for New York before the storm gets worse, or we can put you on something for tomorrow."

I didn't know what to do. Neither seemed workable. The chances that the tomorrow morning flights would make it out of here were slim. I'd just be stuck repeating this day over and over again, trying to get a flight home. "What about another airline? Can you work something out with them? Please."

"Sorry," he said. "There's nothing I can do."

Nothing.

I wasn't going to make it back. I was going to be sitting here in terminal 2 for the rest of the weekend and someone else was going to get their chance at stardom because I missed my shot.

I was *so* over the airport.

EIGHTEEN

Snap out of it, Sari. Not getting home was not an option. It just wasn't.

I marched over to one of the phone stations and dropped my guitar and backpack. I didn't see Fitz anywhere. But I didn't need him; this was on me. I was going to find my own way home. The in-person agent was no help, so I needed to get through to the one on the phone. They wouldn't have dozens of people breathing down their neck. They could focus on me, and that's what I needed.

"Is it okay if I put you on hold for a minute and see if I can come up with anything?" the agent asked after I pleaded my case.

"Sure, that would be great, Deena. Thank you." I had heard using someone's name made them more inclined to help you, and I'd take any advantage I could get. But I wasn't going to let her be my last hope to get home. I needed a backup plan.

I took out my cell and called Trina for help. She knew how important this performance was to me. "I will drive down there and get you myself, if I have to," she said.

I knew she meant it, but even if I had been willing to take

her up on the offer (which I wasn't), there wouldn't be enough time. It was easily a forty-eight-hour-drive here and back. For the first time, I regretted not having a license of my own. Trina had been right on that one. I could have rented a car and been on my way home already. Twenty-four hours of straight driving would have gotten me there with a few hours to spare.

"Can you check the other airlines for me?" I asked her. Just because my carrier was booked up, it didn't mean all the others were, too. Trina pulled out her laptop and got to work searching for flights. I didn't care what it cost. This was crisis time. If there was ever a time for me to use my emergency credit card, it was now. I'd pay my parents back. Even if I had to give guitar lessons to every kid in my neighborhood for the rest of my life to do it.

I had a phone to each ear. I looked ridiculous, but it didn't matter. Not if it got me home.

"Anything?" I asked Trina.

"Not yet," she said.

"How's it looking?"

There was a long pause.

"That good, huh?" I asked.

"I'm sorry," she said. "I'm still trying."

"I know. I appreciate it. Thank you." My phone started to beep. I looked at the caller ID. *Crap.* "Trina, it's my mom. I'm sorry, I have to take it. Text me if you see anything?"

She promised, and I switched over to my mother.

"I just saw your flight was canceled," she said.

"Yeah, I know. I'm trying to figure something out now." I told her about the airline wanting to send me to Detroit.

"No," she said. "I don't want you stuck there. It's already started raining here, and it's supposed to get a lot worse. Why don't you book a flight for Sunday? That way the storm will have passed, and you won't have to go through this again. Your gram will come pick you up."

"I can't. You know I have the show."

"Sari, they'll understand. The weather isn't your fault."

My fists tightened around both phones. I loved my mom, and she was generally pretty supportive, but she just didn't get *how* important this gig was to me. There were no guarantees I'd get another chance. They were giving me a break, and excuses weren't going to cut it. "It doesn't work like that, Mom."

"Do you want me to call them?"

"What? NO!" That would be a great way to be taken seriously—having my mommy call.

"I can say I'm your manager."

If my hands hadn't been filled with phones, I would have pulled my hair out. "Mom, I got this. Don't worry."

"Sari—"

"Miss Silver—"

Both people on both phones started talking to me at once.

"Mom, hang on," I said. "I have the airline on. Deena, go ahead."

"I'm not seeing anything that goes into JFK tonight," Deena said.

I squeezed my eyes shut. "What about LaGuardia or Newark? I'll really take anything."

"Unfortunately, there's nothing there, either. I even checked our partner airlines," she said.

"Can you check one more time? Please. I really need to get

back. Put me in an overhead bin, baggage, anything. I don't care as long as it gets me back."

"There's nothing going back to the New York area."

"Just one more look, please?"

She agreed, but she didn't sound optimistic. She probably wasn't even checking, just waiting a few minutes to come back and say there's still nothing.

"I don't know what I'm going to do." I said it mostly to myself, but my mom answered.

"You'll go back to your gram's and we'll sort this out later."

I didn't answer, just half grumbled–half hissed.

Fitz walked over just then. "Any luck?" he mouthed.

"No. Still trying, but I doubt it. You?"

"Sari," my mom said. "Who are you talking to? Is that Zev?"

She adored my ex-boyfriend. "No, it's someone else. Hang on," I pulled the phone away from my ear.

"Sorry," I told Fitz. "Did you wind up with a flight?"

"Sort of. Going to Boston. I have a friend who's driving back to NYU from there. He said he'd pick me up at Logan and take me with him."

"Lucky. I think I'm going to be stuck here."

"Maybe not. I asked my friend about you. If you can get on the three p.m. Boston flight, he said he'd give you a ride, too."

"Are you serious?!"

"Yeah," he said.

I totally wanted to hug him.

"Sari, Sari, who is that?" My mom's voice was so loud, that it was crystal clear even though the phone was near my side. "What is going on? You are not taking a ride with a stranger, do you hear me?"

I did, but I didn't have any other choice.

I covered the mouthpiece with my hand and smiled at Fitz. "I'd love a ride."

My mom would understand. *Eventually.*

NINETEEN

The agent got back on the line and gave me the expected news that there was no room on flights to New York.

"Actually," I said, "how about Boston. I hear there's a three p.m. flight there."

She put me on hold again, and I cautiously lifted the other phone, the one with my mother freaking out on it, back to my ear.

"Sari, Sari, are you listening to me? Where are you? Answer me this second!" she yelled.

"I'm here, I'm here."

"*Please* tell me you are not serious about driving with two strange men from Boston to New York, in a storm no less," she said.

"They're not strange." At least Fitz wasn't. I really didn't know anything about his friend.

"No," she said. "Conversation over. The answer is no."

"Well . . ." She was going to kill me, but I had to say it. "It's not really your call. I'm eighteen."

"Sari Eliza," she said, pulling out the middle name. "You still live under my roof. You will be grounded through summer. Forget performances. You will not be leaving the apartment for anything but school. You are not doing this."

"Mom," I said, "Please. This is *so* important to me. Fitz is a good guy."

"Yeah, just what do you know about him?"

I smiled at Fitz. This conversation would be easier if he wasn't stranding right there. "His grandpa lives in the same retirement community as Gram. He studies at NYU; he's a junior; he's nice, helpful."

"Sari, are you trying to give me and your father a heart attack?"

I hated when she said things like that. "I'll be fine. I'll give you all of Fitz's information. You can even talk to him if you want." I really hoped she didn't take me up on that part.

"The answer is still no, you are not going. I do not want to hear about my daughter on the ten o'clock news."

"You won't. I promise."

"I said no."

As if I didn't have enough aggravation, Zev was walking toward me.

"Mom, it's no different than me getting in a cab," I told her.

But she didn't agree. "You are *not* traveling alone with two men I don't know."

Then I had an idea. A *bad* idea.

"What if I wasn't?" I asked her.

"Wasn't what?" she asked.

"Alone."

"Sari, what are you talking about now?"

I couldn't believe I was going to say this, but as I watched my ex-boyfriend come closer, I knew it was my only shot. "What if Zev came with me?"

TWENTY

I put my mom on Mute, which she wasn't thrilled about, as the agent reappeared on the phone.

"Good news," she said. "There are seats left on the Boston flight. The storm doesn't hit there 'til a little later, so it's not as busy yet."

"Did you say seats—plural?" I asked.

"Yep."

"That's perfect. I may need two."

The lady put me on hold again, and I turned my attention toward Zev.

"You found a flight?" he asked, resting his arms on the little wall of the phone bank and leaning forward.

"Maybe. I might go to Boston and get a ride back to the city with Fitz."

Zev straightened back up. "Oh."

I twisted the cord from the airport phone around my arm. *"Anyway . . ." Just spit it out, Sari. It's the only way to get what you want.* "If there's room in the car, do you want to come?"

"We can make room," Fitz interjected.

"Really?" I asked.

"Sure, no problem," he said.

Only, I wasn't so sure about that. Zev looked pretty skeptical. I had to convince him to come, and not with an audience. I didn't want to scare Fitz off from riding with the two of us. "Fitz, can you give us a few minutes?"

He nodded and went to grab a seat nearby, and I turned my attention back to Zev. "So will you come?"

He picked at his nail. "I don't get it. *You* want to travel with *me*? Why?"

"I'm being nice, okay? Do you want to come or not?"

He eyed me, trying to figure out what I was hiding. "You wouldn't talk to me all week, told me to get away from you all day, and now you want me on your flight and to go on a road trip with you and the guy you're who-knows-what with? What's going on?"

I didn't have time to play coy. The agent would be back on the phone any second, and I couldn't afford losing these seats. "My mom will only let me go if you come, and I'll do whatever it takes to get back to the city."

"Even ride with me."

"Yes," I conceded.

"And will you be ignoring me the whole time?"

Probably, but I was afraid if I told him that, he'd say no. My pause was answer enough.

"I'll take that as a yes," he said. Then he took his own long dramatic pause. "But . . . I'll go anyway."

"You will?"

He shrugged. "You need to get to your show. I'm not going to be the reason you miss it."

No bribery, no bargains, no anything. Just a yes.

"Thank you," I said, quietly.

He nodded.

"One more thing," I said, tapping the Mute button on my phone and taking my mother off Hold. "My mother wants to talk to you."

I finally got back on with the agent and booked the flight to Boston—for me and Zev—while simultaneously trying to listen to what my ex was saying to my mother.

I caught snippets. There was "I'll be there, Mrs. Silver." "Yeah, right?" "Me too." "It's a big deal." "I'm working on it." "That's why we love her." And a bunch of laughter. I swear my mother could be the president of the We Love Zev Geller Fan Club. That might have been part of why I hadn't told her the reason he and I broke up. It was too hard to talk about, and she liked him so much, that seeing or hearing her disappointment would just make it that much worse. Now she thinks I'm the one to blame. That he and I had a silly fight, and that I refused to hear him out about it.

"Here," he said, handing back my phone. "Your battery is dying."

I had a little power left, but I was going to need to charge it very soon. "Thanks."

We swapped places. I took my mom, and he got on with the agent to confirm he wanted the Boston trip.

"I'm still not thrilled with this, Sari," my mother said. "I want frequent check-ins."

"Okay, I promise. Don't worry, it's all going to work out."

And for a brief moment, I actually thought that was true.

TWENTY-ONE

I'd been at the airport so long, it felt like they should have named it after me. Sari Silver International had a nice ring to it . . . sort of.

I was getting cabin fever. I needed some alone time. Especially since it was my last chance for a while. I was going to be stuck on the flight and then in a car with Zev and Fitz. I wasn't in the mood to make any more small talk than I had to.

I told both guys I was going to get lunch and go over my music. They seemed to understand that I needed space, which I was thankful for. I knew I should put my shoes back on. This was disgusting. I was going to wind up on someone's GroupIt feed as an airport horror story. I would have bought some flip-flops, but the terminal wasn't that big—there weren't any to buy. I had to either suffer or be gross.

I really wanted to go with gross, but I decided to momentarily suffer as I headed to the food court. My stomach was growling. The only things I had put in it today were a sip of a smoothie and another of a Frappuccino, and I was starting to feel it. It was definitely time to eat; I didn't need to add hangry to my list of frustrations.

Unfortunately, my food options, if you could call them that, were not exactly enviable. A lot of airport terminals had a ton of decent places to eat. This was not one of them. There were only three vendors (if you didn't count Starbucks and the concession stand). A pizza place, a smoothie shop, and a deli/burger restaurant. None of them looked appetizing.

I went with the pizza. How badly could they mess that up? The answer was incredibly badly. I took one bite and flung it back on the paper plate. At least I was sitting alone. I'd managed to snag a little table by the checkout when a couple got up, right as I finished paying. It was a good time to call Trina back.

"Wait, let me let me get this straight," she said after I told her what went down, "you are going on a road trip with your ex, a hot NYU guy, and his possibly equally hot friend? Please, please, please live post as it happens. I'd pay to see this."

"I know, right? I could start my own reality show. *The Silver Sagas.*"

"You could even play a few songs for the viewing public. Get your music out there."

That reminded me that I was so unprepared for tomorrow night. "I didn't get to rehearse at all today."

"You'll kill it anyway."

I picked at the pizza. "I'd feel better if I could just run through my set a few times." I thought about doing it here, at the airport, but there were so many people feeling cooped up, someone was bound to say something, and I couldn't take another fight. I was too drained.

"You'll have time tomorrow," she assured me.

"You're right." In the meantime, I'd keep running it in my head. "Zev thinks I should end with 'Living, Loving, You.'"

"It is one of your best. . . ."

It really was. My phone beeped. Ugh. Not now. "Trina, my phone is about to die. I'm sorry to keep doing this to you, but I'll call you back later, okay?"

We hung up, and I fished through my backpack. I had an external charger in there somewhere.

I found it, but unfortunately it was dead. Figures. There were no outlets nearby, but I wasn't ready to give up my nice, private little table. Not yet. My phone still had a tiny bit of power, I'd charge it later. I still had plenty of time left at the airport to do it.

I looked over my set list again. Maybe I should change it up. I had been so sure about it before, but now . . . Leaving off my best song just because it reminded me of my ex seemed so amateurish. I was a musician, I was supposed to channel my emotions. I'd see how I felt tomorrow. I didn't have to decide now.

I quietly sang my songs to myself, tapping the table along with the beat. Even though it wasn't even close to full volume, and it was sans guitar, it still felt nice. At this point, anything that took my mind off the airport, my ex, and all the other things that had gone wrong today was a welcome relief.

"Sari!"

I jolted back, almost falling out of my seat. "Seriously, Zev!" I had not expected someone to be standing over me.

"Sorry, didn't mean to scare you."

I sneered at him. "Well, you did."

"I'm sorry."

"What do you want? I told you I wanted some time alone. You *said* okay."

He crossed his arms. "Hey, I'm just trying to help *you. Your* mom has been texting *me* in a panic. You're not answering your phone."

My mom was texting him? Come on, Mom.

I glanced at my phone. "It's dead." My mom loved hearing from Zev so much, what was one more text? "Can you just tell her I need to charge my phone, and I'll get in touch with her after?"

He nodded.

I looked around the food court. All the outlets were taken. I let out a sigh, took my shoes back off (yes, there were a few disgusted stares, which I totally understood. Yet, the idea of walking in those shoes seemed a lot worse than the nastiness of not wearing them), and grabbed my stuff. So much for my private little table. I needed to do something about my phone. I wandered around the gates. All the outlets and charge stations were taken there, too. I shouldn't have been surprised, with so many people's flights delayed, of course they'd grab all the good spots.

So annoying. Especially with Zev at my heels. "You don't need to keep following me."

"It's just in case your mom writes back."

"Uh-huh." We both knew he was full of it. I stared at the nearest charging station. All the plugs were, of course, taken. "This is hopeless."

Zev rubbed his hand on his chin. "If you only knew someone who had an external charger, someone who would share with you, *hmmm*, I wonder who that could be?"

"Good point," I said, ignoring his very unsubtle hint, "Fitz may have one. I'll check."

"What is with you and him?" Zev asked, fidgeting back and forth. "You don't like him, do you?"

I shrugged. I didn't owe him an explanation, no matter how sad he looked or how big the puppy dog eyes he was giving me were. He was the one who kissed someone else. It wasn't my job to make him feel better.

I had no luck with Fitz. He offered to let me use his phone, but he couldn't help me with mine. So I continued on my hunt, Zev still trailing me like a puppy.

"Excuse me," I said to a guy in a suit who had both his laptop and his phone plugged in. "Can I borrow one of the outlets for just a few minutes? My phone is completely dead."

The guy actually said no. He didn't even offer an explanation. He just went right back to using his laptop screen. He didn't care about my phone, as long as he had his. The airport clearly brought out the best in people.

"So you're really going to keep bugging strangers rather than just use my charger?" Zev asked.

"Yep." Now the question was, who to ask? I eyed the crowd. Who looked friendly? No more suits. The people with headphones on wouldn't want to be bothered. There was a woman knitting whose phone was charging. Maybe her?

"Hi," I said, squeezing my way by everyone's bags to get to her. "Beautiful sweater. Great color. I love blue. I was wondering if I could ask you a favor." She looked at me skeptically, like I was going to beg for money or ask her to smuggle a package onto her flight. "My phone died, and I was wondering if I could use your outlet for a little bit. Just enough so I can text home. I have my own charger; I'll leave the phone here; you won't have to get up or anything."

"Oh," she said, "yeah, I guess that would be all right."

Yes!

I handed her my phone and charger to switch out with hers, but the woman seated next to her gave me the look of death. "I've been waiting for a plug for hours," she said. "I'm next."

I wanted to explain that it would just be a few minutes, enough to text my mother, but I could tell she wouldn't want to hear it. I didn't when the lady cut in front of me and Fitz to talk to the agent. Maybe this was karma.

The knitting woman gave me back my phone with a look of apology. "Sorry."

"It's okay. I appreciate you trying. Thanks, anyway," I said.

I went to the next gate with a whole different crew of passengers, preparing to beg all over again, when Zev dangled his external charger in front of my face. "Look at it right here for the taking," he said.

I knew I was being ridiculously stubborn, but I pushed it away and squatted by a guy sitting on the ground next to an outlet. "Excuse me," I tried again. "Can I plug in my phone for a few minutes?"

He snorted. "Use his," he said, jutting his chin up toward my ex-boyfriend who was still hovering, charger in hand.

I stood back up and glared at Zev. "You are making this difficult," I hissed. Was his new mission in life to torture me? Didn't he understand that I didn't want any more favors from him? I already felt like I owed him something for coming to Boston with me, I didn't want to be more in his debt than I had to be. My insides were shredded enough from having to spend all this time with him. I didn't know how much more I could take.

"It doesn't have to be," Zev said. "You can just use the charger." He moved it back and forth in front of me like a pendulum on a grandfather clock.

If he thought he was charming, he was wrong. "Fine, you win," I said, as I reached up to grab it. Only Zev pulled it away.

"Not so fast," he countered. "This one is gonna cost you."

I raised an eyebrow. "You're kidding me." I knew something like this was coming.

"'Fraid not."

I rolled my eyes. He really was the devil, and now he was making me sell my soul—and my sanity. "What's your price?"

"Just to talk." He tossed the charger up and caught it in his palm, to taunt me. "I think that's fair."

"Fine whatever, just give it to me." I didn't have much choice. If I didn't figure out a way to get in touch with my mom soon, Zev would remain the go-between, and that would be even worse.

"Promise we can talk?"

"I do," I conceded.

He handed it over, and I plugged my phone in.

Then we just stood there, awkwardly facing each other, waiting for my phone to charge. "Sari," he finally said, his face getting all serious. "About Bethanne—"

"No, not now."

"You said we could talk."

I shook my head. "I didn't mean in the middle of the airport." We were right around gobs of people, the grouch who wouldn't give me his charger, families, couples, random others. They didn't need to hear my drama. "I'd like at least the illusion of privacy."

"Fine," he said, and gestured toward his suitcase. "You might as well have a seat while we wait."

"On *that*? Are you kidding? I'll crush it."

"You will not," he said. "Just sit. It beats standing around the airport barefoot."

He did have a point, and I *was* getting tired, so I agreed. "Fine."

A moment later, I was falling backward. "What the . . . ?!"

"Just relax," Zev said. He had tilted the suitcase to a forty five-degree angle and was starting to roll it, *and me*, across the terminal.

"My stuff!"

"It's right here," he said. I looked back. He was wearing my backpack and had my guitar case in one hand as he pushed me along.

"This is crazy. Where are we going, Zev?!" I was grasping the sides of the suitcase. "I'm going to fall."

"I got you," he said.

This was ridiculous. "Where are you taking me?"

"You said you didn't want to talk in the middle of the airport, so I'm giving you your illusion of privacy."

And causing a spectacle as he did it. The random barefoot girl being pushed around on a suitcase got more than her fair share of raised eyebrows and head shakes as Zev and I made our way through the crowd.

He put me upright once we got to the corner of the terminal. There were still people around, but we had a little section to ourselves.

I jumped up. "That was not funny."

"I wasn't trying to be funny. I'm just trying to talk to you. What I've been trying to do all week. And you promised."

I took a deep breath and exhaled slowly. "All right, then. Go ahead. Talk."

TWENTY-TWO

Zev fidgeted as I stood there, hands on hips, waiting for what he had to say. "Well?" I questioned.

He seemed to be trying to find the right words, but I was pretty sure there were no right words for *I betrayed you*.

"I'm sorry, Sari. I never meant to hurt you. I love you."

"Funny way of showing it," I said. Too smugly, no doubt.

"Please, let me get this out, then you can say whatever you need to. I just want to explain. *She* kissed *me*. I would never have done that to you."

I bit my lip. It was taking every ounce of willpower not to interrupt him.

"I was just caught off guard. That's it, I promise. It was just a second. When you walked in—"

I couldn't stay quiet. "*When I walked in* is when you *stopped*. So you want me to believe I just had such impeccable timing that I got there at the exact moment she planted her lips on yours and you hadn't been going at it beforehand?"

He took a step toward me. "We weren't. I promise."

I countered by taking a step back. "That's quite the coincidence."

"I don't know, maybe Bethanne saw you come in, and that's why she swooped in at that exact moment."

"So you finally admit she *does* want you back?" I shook my head. I had been telling him that for months. She had started dropping by our table at lunch, but never to say hello to me, she'd pop up at his improv shows, and of course liked every single thing he posted online—unless I was in it—but Zev kept telling me I was reading too much into everything, and that she just wanted to stay friends.

"Yeah, but I didn't know," he said.

My hands flew off my hips and into the air. "I *told* you."

"I thought you were being—"

He stopped himself.

"*Jealous?*" I asked. "What I should have been was smart. I should have known something was going to happen."

He was picking at his nails so hard, I thought he might draw blood. "Nothing happened."

"I. Saw. You. You were with her. You wanted *her.*"

I squeezed my eyes shut.

When I opened them back up, Zev was standing closer. "No. I didn't. And I don't. It wasn't like that," he said, his voice softer.

"Then what was it like, Zev?" I said, matching his lower volume. "A whole party full of people and you spent the entire night with your ex. An ex who dumped you, an ex you loved, an ex who hates me and wants you back. Tell me, how am I supposed to feel? What am I supposed to think?"

"You're supposed to trust me."

"I did, and you kissed HER." I shook my head. "I don't even understand why you were you hanging out with her in the first place. She's awful. How could the same person who says they like me ever have liked *her*? Bethanne and I are opposites."

He sighed. "Not completely. I know you don't want to hear this, but she's not all bad."

He was right, I *really* didn't want to hear this. It hurt hearing him come to her defense, but I held my tongue, and he kept talking. "She's funny, she goes after what she wants, she's great with animals—even volunteers at a shelter, and she's really loyal to her friends."

I gave him a skeptical look, but he continued. "She wanted to stay friends after we broke up, but I didn't." They had ended things April of sophomore year. "I told you how my dad had a heart attack that summer," he said.

I nodded.

"Well, Bethanne called me every day to check on me, she even babysat my sister so my mom and I could go to the hospital." His sister was ten years younger than him. "She was there for me. I haven't forgotten that. I don't want her back, I didn't even back then, but I thought maybe she and I could make it as friends. She was there when I needed someone, I guess it helped me overlook some of the bad stuff. But I should have listened to you when you told me what she was up to."

"You never told me she did that," I said.

"She wasn't exactly your favorite subject. But you have to believe me. I didn't want to kiss her. I was just . . . I was caught off guard. I was going to stop it, that's when you came in. Honest. I know how that sounds, but it's the truth."

"I don't know."

This time, he was the one to shake his head. "How can you

not know? I'm trying here, Sari. What I don't get is how you don't trust me. You know how I feel about you."

"And I know how you felt about *her*." Zev was my first love, but I wasn't his. There was nothing he could do about that, but I hated it anyway. It made what happened last week with Bethanne even worse.

"That was ages ago," he said, his eyes focused on me, "and what I feel for you is so much stronger."

I stared at my feet. This was so much to take in. Was he telling the truth? I didn't know. I saw him kiss her. I knew how much he liked her. I saw the GroupIt posts. I'd been humiliated. "If Bethanne didn't break it off, you'd probably still be together right now. We might not have really known each other back then, but I knew about your breakup. Everyone did. All anyone could talk about was how she crushed you." I glanced back up at him.

He was rubbing his temples. "I don't know what I'm supposed to say to that, Sari. Yeah, I was hurt when she dumped me. Yeah, I moped around. Yeah, I wanted her back."

Zev and I had never really talked about Bethanne. Other than me saying she wanted him back, we never really got into their relationship or what happened or anything like that. Hearing it now, reminded me why. It was as if he took one of my shoes and stabbed me repeatedly in the gut with the heel.

"But that was *then*," he continued. "I got over it, I moved on, I went out with other people, then I met you. I fell in love with *you*, and it's not like anything I ever felt before. Bethanne isn't the one I want back, *you* are."

I wanted to believe that was true.

"She knew about our breakup, Zev. If you wanted me back,

why would you spread that? I hadn't told people we were over, but *she* knew. *You* told her."

"I told her I didn't want anything to do with her anymore. I called her the morning after the party to tell her to quit texting me, that I didn't want to hear from her anymore. And when she asked why, I said that after what she did at the party, I lost you, and that I was going to do whatever it took to get you back. And that included not hanging out with her anymore."

I studied his eyes. Was he telling me the truth? I wasn't sure. "Really?"

"Yes. She's out of my life. I told her. I should have done it sooner. I should have listened to you. I'm sorry, Sari. Please tell me we're okay, that you forgive me."

Memories good and bad were crowding my mind. Zev's lips on Bethanne. Zev's lips on mine. Reading the comments on Bethanne's post. The stories of when they broke up. The night Zev asked me out. The time we went to his family's lake house and accidentally fell asleep on the neighbor's dock and freaked out his parents. The time he raced back to my apartment to get my lucky guitar pick because I forgot it and needed it for my performance. The first time he told me he loved me—I had been crying after getting kicked out of band—he totally made me forget all about it.

"I need to think," I said. "I need some time, Zev. Time alone."

He didn't say anything; he just nodded, lifted the handle on his carry-on, and walked off, dragging the suitcase behind him. He didn't look back.

I wasn't sure if I was relieved or disappointed.

TWENTY-THREE

Fitz was sitting on the ground with his back against the wall. I joined him. He had his headphones on and was reading some philosophy textbook.

"Get your phone charged?" he asked.

I nodded. "Now I think I'm just going to relax and listen to some music." That was my hint that I did not feel like talking.

Fitz seemed to get it. He went back to his book and left me alone, but I still wasn't able to relax. All I could think about was what Zev said. Maybe it was all a big misunderstanding. But what if it wasn't? If someone other than Zev had tried to kiss me, I'd have pushed them away and said, "What the hell?" in a fraction of a second. He had lingered.

I gnawed at my lip. Was it possible he had just been completely caught off guard?

I debated it with myself for the next half hour—until Zev himself came over.

He held up his hands. "I'm not following you. It's just getting close to boarding and this is the gate, but I can go sit over there."

I patted the floor next to me. "You can stay."

For the next few minutes Fitz, Zev, and I pretty much sat there in silence. That is until I saw Zev typing away on his phone. I peeked to see who he was writing to. For a brief moment I thought maybe it was Bethanne, but the name I saw at the top of the screen surprised me even more.

"Are you still texting with my *mother*?"

"Yeah, she wants to know what's going on," he said.

"She can ask *me*."

"I guess she likes talking to me," he answered.

I shook my head. "Stop texting my mom. It's weird."

He kept typing. "Uh-uh. One Silver woman still likes me; I'm not jeopardizing that."

This was beyond bizarre. I didn't know how I felt about Zev, if I was forgiving him or not, I didn't need my mom getting in the middle.

I texted her:

> Quit texting Zev.

> **MOM**
> He answers me. You don't.

This was not happening.

> I'm answering you right now!!!

I saw three little dots pop up on my phone. It meant she was typing. Only no message appeared. Then I looked over at Zev. He was laughing. Was my mom still messaging him?!

Really?!

I texted Zev:

> Knock it off.

> **VOLDEMORT**
> Nope.

I didn't know whether to laugh or scream.

> If you don't quit it,
> I'll start texting your mom.

> **VOLDEMORT**
> Go ahead. Tell her I say hi. ;)

I thrust my head back against the wall, but Zev just smiled at me, that little dimple popping up above his cheek, at least it did until he saw my phone and how his name appeared. "Hey, why does that say Voldemort?" he said, his voice filled with mock outrage. "I'm much more a Harry."

"A *Harry*—really?"

"Okay maybe a Cedric," he said, referring to the heroic, handsome one.

"Try a Weasley. You'd totally be one of the twins always try-ing to stir things up."

"Brilliant prankster? I'll take it."

I couldn't help but laugh. Sitting there, joking with Zev, it felt like old times. In that moment, I forgot about Bethanne. I forgot about our fight. I forgot we broke up. Then his knee accidentally brushed up against my leg and that familiar touch made it all come crashing back, all those memories of him and his ex pressed together, while I was just standing there. My whole body felt numb.

I wanted to forgive Zev. I really did. I just wasn't sure I could.

TWENTY-FOUR

"Ladies and gentlemen, at this time we'd like to begin our boarding for flight 2043 to Boston," a voice announced over the loudspeaker.

"It's a miracle!!" My prison sentence at the airport was over, I was being released. They finally, finally, *finally* called my flight. It was time to go home. Well, Boston, and then home. But close enough! "I don't think I could have taken it much longer. Thank God we're getting out of here."

"It wasn't that bad," Fitz said, standing up.

He had no idea. I put the heels of torture back on and got to my feet, trying to focus on the relief of going home instead of the cruel punishment my toes were facing. "Yes, it was." I joined the group of people hovering by the gate ready to make a sprint for the door as soon as their zone was called. Fitz and Zev followed. "We're like caged animals here," I told him. "Worse. This is like one of those sadistic experiments where they trap you in an enclosed place with a bunch of other people and watch how you respond, waiting to see how long it takes until you crack. And from the looks of this crowd, it won't be much longer."

"Tell us how you really feel," Zev said.

He probably did *not* want me to do that. The betrayal, hurt, and confusion I felt were still at the forefront of my mind.

"I am just calling it like I see it," I said instead.

"Well," Fitz said, "on the upside, you did get to see me again."

"Yeah, like she said," Zev mumbled, so that only I'd hear him, "the day was torture."

I elbowed him. He could be jealous all he wanted, but Fitz had figured out how to get me back to New York, and I wouldn't forget that. I guess not *everyone* at the airport was worried only about themselves.

"That is true," I said. I couldn't see Zev behind me, but I could almost imagine his eyes rolling all the way to the back of his head.

The people with small children and those who needed extra time boarded, then zone one was called.

"That's me," Fitz said. He was lucky, I was in the last zone. "I'll see you on the plane. Maybe we can even get seats together."

I nodded. "Sounds perfect."

"*Perfect*," Zev mimicked as Fitz walked away from us.

"Quit it," I said, turning to face him, "Fitz is doing me a huge favor. Stop acting like a five-year-old."

"Okay, I'm sorry, but quit pretending you're into him."

"Who said I was pretending?"

His eyes bore into mine. "I did. Because I know you still love me as much I love you. That doesn't go away just because you want it to."

I wanted him to be wrong.

"Love isn't everything," I said.

He shook his head, his eyes still on mine. "Yes, it is."

Stop it, Zev. I didn't want to think about him or love. I broke his gaze. If love was everything, it was everything that was wrong with me right now. It was why my heart felt like someone put a clamp on it and was squeezing tighter and tighter, making it almost impossible to breathe. It was why I felt like a shadow was living inside of me. It was why I felt like screaming, crying, and huddling in a tiny ball while I rocked myself back and forth. Nothing might be the answer, because I wasn't sure I could take Zev back, and as much as Trina wanted it to be the case, not even flirting with a hot NYU guy had numbed the pain I was feeling.

I grabbed Zev's ticket to check his seat number: 30C. I breathed a sigh of relief. I was 25A. I could not handle a whole flight next to him. I wasn't ready for that yet. I still needed to figure everything out.

"Wait," I said, reexamining his ticket. "You're zone one boarding. You could have gotten on the plane already. Why didn't you? They're already on zone two. Go."

He shook his head. "I'm not going to leave you here."

"I'm fine."

"I know."

Damn it. It was the little things like that that were going to be my undoing. "Really," I said, "you don't need to wait for me."

"What would your mom say," he said, with mock outrage. Then he pulled out his phone and proceeded to text her:

> We're about to board.

"You are such a kiss-up."

"Whatever works," he said. That dimpled smile of his appeared again, and I couldn't stop myself, I smiled back.

My zone was called and we got in line. I had been waiting so I'd be the first one to board, but I wasn't the only one with that idea. I wound up about sixth.

"Some of you are going to have to check your bags," the agent said. "You'll be able to pick them up right as you deplane."

This was bad. *Very* bad.

"I really need to keep my guitar with me," I told her, once I got to the front. I could not leave Ruby. She was my prized possession. There was no way I could risk her getting stolen or damaged. I'd be panicked by the thought on a normal day, but with my performance tomorrow? This was major.

"I'll check mine so she can keep hers," Zev said.

"I'm sorry, but you're both going to need to do it. Everyone from this point on is." She handed us little pink tags to wrap around the handles.

"Please," I said. "I'm begging you. Can I just try and see if I can find a spot? This is like my baby."

She let out a sigh. "You can ask the flight attendants. See what they say."

I thanked her as she scanned my ticket.

Zev and I walked down the pathway to the plane. Well, he walked. I hobbled. My feet had swollen, and walking in these nightmare shoes was hellish. I was more concerned about Ruby than my feet, though.

"Try to hide the guitar between us when we board," he said.

I nodded. He dropped his suitcase by the open door for

loading and then got on the flight. I was practically on top of him, trying to use our bodies to hide my case.

I actually made it to my row before I had a problem.

Zev and I opened just about every bin around us checking for room. There wasn't any.

"Excuse me," the flight attendant said. "You're going to need to check that."

"Please, no." Ruby was my everything. I couldn't have her go under the plane. The airline lost luggage all the time. My last trip it took my mom two days to get her bag back and my dad's was never found. "This guitar is my life. I can't stow her."

"Miss, you don't have a choice," he said. "All the bins are taken."

"Please."

"Miss . . . ," he said again.

Zev put his hand on my arm. "I think you might have to, Sari."

I just stood there. I was at a loss. There was nothing I could do. If I kept fighting with the flight attendant and made a scene, I would be kicked off with Ruby. If I didn't, I risked losing my guitar. I wanted to cry. Why couldn't anything go right?

"Maybe I can help."

It was Fitz.

He was two rows back. He stood up and moved into the aisle. "My bag is taking up one of those bins. I'll check it, so she can put her guitar in."

The flight attendant said okay, and after Fitz handed him his bag and did a little bit of rearranging of a jacket and a backpack that were also in there, Ruby fit right in.

"Fitz, thank you. Thank you, thank you, thank you." It was official. He *was* Captain America. "You are my hero."

"I tried to do the same thing," Zev pointed out, but I ignored him.

"It wasn't a big deal," Fitz said.

"It was to me."

"Please take your seats," the flight attendant said, breaking up my gush fest.

As I turned to head to 25A, the woman in Fitz's row called out to me. "Are you two together? You can have my seat, I'll take yours," she offered.

"Really?" I asked.

She nodded. "A cute couple like you shouldn't have to sit apart."

"Thank you, that would be great."

Zev was still standing there. I could see his muscles tense. But what did he want me to do? Explain my messed-up social life to a stranger on a plane? It wasn't like I was choosing Fitz over him. It was Fitz or a stranger. And the thought of being near a friend right now seemed nice.

The woman scooted out of her window seat, and I moved in.

I instantly felt the stress start to drain away.

All was good. I was going home.

TWENTY-FIVE

I was beginning to rethink my seat change. Fitz was stocky. Wide shoulders and giant arms, which both made their way into my space. My hips, on the other hand, ran into his. We were like inverted triangles, pressed up close to each other, and not in a fun, flirty way. It was uncomfortable. Fitz's upper body was taking up a quarter of my seat. I tried to scrunch my arms together and make myself smaller to give us more room, but I couldn't exactly change the laws of physics. It didn't help that my limited legroom was taken by my backpack. But I'd take the uncomfortable seat, the knees hitting the back of the chair in front of me, and the stale air surrounding me, because at least I was on the plane!

A plane that hadn't moved in what seemed like forever.

"Ladies and gentlemen, I'm sorry for the delay," the flight attendant said over the loudspeaker. "We are eighth in line for takeoff. In preparation, if you could please make sure your seat belts are securely fastened and all carry-on bags are stowed underneath the seat in front of you or in the overhead bins. Make sure your seat backs and tray tables are in the full upright position. We'll be coming by to check, and then going over some safety instructions."

Eighth for takeoff? We'd be on the tarmac a long time. Hopefully not long enough for Boston to cancel the flight.

A few minutes later, the plane started to move, but I was under no illusions. It was just getting in place. We weren't close to taking off.

"Sir, I need you to sit back and put on your seat belt," the flight attendant was saying to someone. "We can't take off until you do, and I'm sure you don't want to be responsible for us losing our place in line."

"He's hyperventilating," someone else said.

"What now?" I asked. I couldn't see. Fitz and the people behind me were blocking my view, but it sounded like some passenger was risking our chance of getting out of here. They needed to calm down—now.

"Whoa," Fitz said, turning back to me. "It's your friend. He's freaking out."

Crap. I took off my seat belt and stood up. Zev was doubled over and looked like he was having trouble breathing. I knew he had issues flying, but I hadn't expected this. We weren't even in the air, the plane was barely moving, and he was already a wreck.

"Let me out," I said to Fitz.

He stood, and I ungracefully—tragically so—attempted to scoot past him. Fitz had moved toward the back of the plane (where I needed to be) instead of toward the front, and I couldn't fit past him. After a little dance number where we unsuccessfully tried to switch places, he moved back into his seat, and I made it to Zev's row. Only I wasn't greeted with open arms.

"Miss, I need you to sit down," the flight attendant said.

"I know. I'm with him. I can help."

"She can have my seat," the guy next to Zev offered, jumping up. He had been scrunched up against the window, probably afraid Zev would throw up on his shoes.

"Come on, Zev," I said, and helped him stand up. "Let the man out. I'm going to sit with you."

He stood, and I had an image of Bambi learning to walk. He seemed so fragile. I hated seeing him like this. It broke my heart—well, in an entirely different way than before, but it still hurt. All I wanted at that moment was to help him.

We sat back down, and the flight attendant brought over my bag.

"Hey," I said, putting my hand on Zev's back and rubbing it. "Look out the window; we're not even taking off yet. The plane is just getting in position. It's not time to panic yet."

Zev looked over and stared at the tarmac for a bit. Finally, he spoke. "So you'll let me know when it is?" His breathing was still ragged, but it was starting to come back to normal.

"Yes," I said, "when I start screaming, you can freak out."

The corner of his mouth crept up into a slight smile. "Like on the roller coaster?"

"Exactly." I loved roller coasters, but I always screamed about ten seconds before the descent. It was the anticipation of the fall that I found the scariest. Zev would always tell me my shrieks were more panic inducing than the ride. "But," I said, giving him the side eye, "if you can handle Kingda Ka at Great Adventure, this should be nothing."

"I know." His eyes stayed focused on the window. I guess he

wanted to make sure we really were still on the ground. "I don't know what it is about planes; it's just different."

"You've been in cab rides way bumpier than this is going to be," I said. That may have been an exaggeration, but if it got him to calm down, I didn't care.

Zev shrugged. "I told you I was a terrible flier."

Then I remembered, the only reason he was on a plane at all was because of me. "How did you handle the flight down here?"

"It wasn't as bad. I took something."

"Um," I said, my eyes bugging out at him, "why aren't you taking something now?"

He rubbed his lids underneath his glasses. "I was in a rush to pack and get to the airport, I didn't want to miss you. The pills wound up in the other suitcase, and I didn't realize it until it was already checked."

Zev had always been a last-minute packer. I could picture him tossing everything into his bag minutes before he left this morning. Now he was paying for that.

For the moment, he seemed to be doing okay, but that was bound to change. If he lost it that much from the plane just moving a bit, takeoff was going to be a challenge.

We sat there in silence. He clutched the armrests as the plane moved forward, but he kept his cool, at least until the plane started taxiing thirty minutes later. I felt the vibration as the wheels made their way down the runway, picking up speed, until the plane began liftoff. Zev's eyes got wide as he stared out the window, watching the runway, the planes, the buildings miniaturize below.

"Look down," I told him.

That stomach-sinking sensation that happens as the plane

climbs higher washed through me. I actually found it a little exhilarating. This time more than ever. It meant I was finally getting out of Florida, but what was thrilling for me was making Zev sick. He was hunched over again, staring at his feet, his hands now on the seat in front of him, and the heavy breathing had returned.

"You okay?" I asked.

"Yup," he said, between painfully deep breaths.

He clearly wasn't. I took the barf bag from the seat pocket and handed it to him. "Breathe in and out of this," I instructed him.

He didn't ask questions or protest, he just did it.

The plane seemed to be cruising now, but there was still a little turbulence, and Zev was Casper the Friendly Ghost white.

"Remember when we got lost trying to find our way to the Cloisters?" I asked him, trying to take his mind off things. It's a museum in Upper Manhattan surrounded by a few acres of land. "The sun was brutal, and I didn't think we were ever going to make it out of there."

He pulled the bag away from his face. "I remember." His breathing was still heavier than usual but calmer than it was a few minutes ago.

"But you got us out of there. You stayed focused and found us the path to the museum. We were fine."

He nodded.

"We'll be fine now, too," I said. "I'll help you get through this."

He took another deep breath into the bag and looked up at me, trying to smile. "Are you going to sing to me?" He took another couple of breaths, " 'Summer Nights'?"

The thought of the song and the memories associated with it stabbed at my heart. "That only works with a partner."

"I'm always game."

That was true. "Where's a karaoke machine when you need one?" I asked.

"The JCC."

That was where Zev and I first got together. It was a Hanukkah party. He was there with his friends, and I was there with mine. There was karaoke, which I could never pass up. I was begging my friends—any of them—to do the duet from the movie *Grease* with me. They all refused. Zev had been standing nearby. He jumped in and offered to sing with me.

"At least now you know the tune," I said.

He pulled the bag away again. "I would have done anything to get you to notice me, even humiliate myself." The talking seemed to be helping his breathing.

I bumped my shoulder lightly into his and laughed. "And that you did."

When we got up onstage, it became evident *very* quickly that Zev didn't know the song *at all*. He wasn't even close to belting out the right tune. But he didn't stop, he kind of talked/ made up his own music throughout the whole thing. Right after, when I asked him why he volunteered if he didn't know the song, he gave me this big goofy grin, with that little dimple of his, and said he wanted an "in" to talk to me.

I was totally charmed.

"The look on your face when I told you I never saw *Grease*," he said, gripping the armrest tight as we hit a tiny bit of turbulence, "was priceless."

"It's a classic," I protested. "And you did improv. Anyone in any aspect of the theater should have seen it. But your response was pretty smooth, I'll give you that."

After my mock horror, he said that I was right, that he should see it, and invited me to his apartment to watch it together.

He smiled at that. "Yeah, it was, until you scrunched up your face and asked me if I had just invited you to Netflix and chill."

"You started stammering. 'Wh-what? No, no, that's not what I meant.'"

"Then you laughed."

"And you said, 'not that I'd object, but I'm just looking for any excuse to hang around you.'"

I told him he didn't need an excuse, and then we sat down at a little table and spent the rest of the night talking. By the time the party ended, I was pretty sure I was in love. I had never believed in the instant connection, butterflies in the stomach, flutter of the heart stuff that people always wrote about. But in that moment, I did.

I studied his face now. He seemed calmer, like he almost forgot where we were, and I almost—key point being *almost*—forgot how much I wanted to be done with him.

"I'd wanted to talk to you since I first saw you perform," he said. We had both been part of the school talent show junior year, but we didn't really hang out. He was usually in the lighting booth, and I was down in the auditorium. I noticed him, I mean he was Zev Geller, but we didn't otherwise cross paths. "I couldn't take my eyes off you."

"Well, that was your job," I reminded him. "You were in charge of the spotlight."

"You didn't need it; you shone without it."

"Okay," I said, "the altitude is messing with your head. That was super cheesy."

I said the wrong thing. Reminding him that we were high aboveground made him gulp for air, but he kept talking. "No, it's true, Sari. You're always beautiful, but when you're onstage, you light up."

The look in his eye was pretty convincing. It made me want to forgive him, but I still wasn't sure that was the smart thing to do. I needed to stop going down memory lane with him. It was messing with my mind. I needed to think *without* Zev in my ear.

"Where's your phone?" I asked him.

He pulled it out, and I punched up a playlist I had made him earlier this year. "Close your eyes and listen to this," I said. "Maybe you can actually get some sleep." And I'd get some time to sort out what I was feeling.

I watched him as he sat there, leaning back against the headrest.

He looked so sweet, so peaceful. I felt the urge to put my head on his shoulder. Being near him, even today, even when I was pissed, still felt right. Did that mean I should give him a second chance?

Zev did have a good explanation for what happened, and he was super believable when he said he was done with Bethanne. Throwing out everything we had because she kissed him might have been an overreaction. Still . . . the way that made me feel was the worst thing I'd ever gone through. I wasn't about to forget it anytime soon, but maybe there was a way to get past it.

I could take things slow. I didn't have to jump back in right where Zev and I left off. I could test the waters, see if we could get back to what we had. He'd never done anything like this before, so didn't he deserve the benefit of the doubt?

I studied his chest and found myself matching my breathing with his. In and out. In and out. In and out.

Zev still had a piece of my heart, and from everything he said, it sounded like I still had a piece of his—and I wasn't ready to give it up.

There was still confusion, there was still hurt, there was still distrust, but there was also longing and more important—love.

If I was being honest with myself, I missed him. I wanted him back.

I put my head on his shoulder. His breathing changed again, only this time it felt like a sigh of relief.

It felt right.

TWENTY-SIX

I jolted upright. *Where was I?* The plane. I must have fallen asleep. My jerking motion stirred Zev awake.

"Sorry," I said, getting my bearings back. My eyelids were heavy and my mouth felt dry and sticky. I reached into my bag and took out some gum and handed a piece to Zev. "It will help during the landing, to pop your ears."

"Thanks."

His face looked ashen. "You'll be fine," I assured him.

"Yeah," he said, "it's just knowing the landing is coming. The flight attendant just came by to collect the trash. That's what woke you."

"You weren't sleeping?" I asked, trying to suppress a yawn.

He shook his head. "Was just closing my eyes."

I rolled my neck to get the kinks out. "You seem to be doing okay."

"Having you on my shoulder helped. Didn't want to risk waking you."

"I'm a pretty sound sleeper."

He winked. "I know." When we accidentally fell asleep on his neighbor's dock last summer, I didn't hear the search party screaming our names until Zev literally shook me awake.

I took a deep breath. It was time to clue him in that I was considering letting us get back to being *us*. "Thanks for letting me borrow your shoulder." I kept my eyes on my knees. "It felt nice."

"You can use it whenever you want it," he said. "In fact, the whole car ride home, it's yours."

"Maybe I'll take you up on that."

"You will?"

I glanced up at him. "Yeah. I mean, if that's okay."

He was nodding so much he looked like one of those bobbleheads they give out at baseball games. "Sari, does this mean . . ." His voice trailed off.

"It means I'm not ruling anything out. I'm still angry, but you're right, it wasn't all your fault, and maybe we can work through it."

"I'll do anything, Sari. *Anything.*"

"*Anything?* Okay. How about for starters," I said, wiggling my eyebrows up and down, "don't freak out on landing."

"That's not fair," he said, throwing his hand over his heart, like I had stabbed him. "You know I have no control over that."

"I know," I said, "I'm kidding. I would never hold that against you. But try not to get us kicked off the plane, okay? I really don't want to have to deal with security."

He held up his fingers in the Boy Scout pledge. "I'll do my best."

"Good, and I'll be here for you," I said.

"Yeah?" he asked.

"Yeah." Our eyes locked, and despite everything going on, I actually felt happy.

A voice came through the speaker. "Hello, everyone, this is your pilot. We are cleared for landing. The weather may make this a little bumpy, but we'll get you home safe and sound."

"I hope so," Zev said under his breath as he grasped the armrests.

"We'll be fine." I meant more than just the landing.

The plane began to descend.

"Hang in there," I told him.

"I'm okay," Zev said through gritted teeth.

He definitely didn't look okay.

"We're almost there." The plane went down a little and then back up, like it was shaking. "Don't worry, it's nothing," I said. Then it happened again.

He gave me a terse smile. "Yep," he said. He was trying to act chill, but fear was permeating his voice.

"Just a little turbulence." But it was more than a little. Out the window I could barely make out the buildings below, and the rain was coming down so hard, it wasn't making this landing easy. The plane jolted and my stomach dropped. Zev went even more pallid, and his breathing was getting heavy.

He started picking at his nails, which were already a mess.

I took his hand. "I got you."

He held on to me tightly. Our fingers were intertwined, and his palm felt warm against mine. I found myself breathing a little shallower, too, but for different reasons. I was really doing this, I was getting back together with Zev. I looked at our clasped hands. His palms were almost double the size of mine, but somehow they fit perfectly.

I kept a firm grip, trying to steady him, to quell his shaking.

When Zev gasped at the next bump, I massaged my thumb against his. "Almost there."

The wheels hit the tarmac with a thud. "We're on the ground," I said, giving Zev's hand one final squeeze before letting go. "We made it."

"Thank you," he said. His hazel eyes looked almost green, and so warm.

"You're welcome." He was still trembling a little, which was actually kind of endearing. I turned my phone on. "I better text my mother, let her know we made it before she bombards you with texts. She probably already did."

"I'll check," he said, turning off airplane mode on his cell.

"There are a ton of messages," he said, and I turned to watch as alert after alert popped up on his screen. He lifted the phone closer to him, but he was still shaky and wound up dropping it.

"I got it."

I took off my seat belt and bent down to pick it up.

No. No, no, no, no, NO.

Ice ran through my veins. His phone almost painful to the touch. This was *not* happening. It wasn't. But it *was*. Everything Zev had told me was a lie.

The evidence was right in my hands; evidence that I was an idiot.

The last alert Zev got was still visible on his screen. It was a text. A text from Bethanne. A text that would be seared into my brain forever. A text that said:

> **BETHANNE**
> See you tomorrow night. XOXO.

TWENTY-SEVEN

Wow. I really *was* gullible. Fool me once, shame on you. Fool me twice, shame on me. But a third time? How did I even manage to get accepted into college? It clearly wasn't because of my street smarts. I fell for every single line that Zev fed me. So much for cutting Bethanne out of his life. He wasn't just still texting her, he was planning to *hang out* with her.

He lied, and I believed him.

I was so pissed. At him, but more so at myself. I should have known better. Zev was amazing at spinning things. The way he charmed the guy with the Harry Potter book should have tipped me off. I don't know why I thought I'd be immune to his alternative facts.

I handed him his phone without saying a word.

"Thanks," he said. "You were right; your mom did text."

I ignored him.

"Sari?"

I stood up, and moved out into the aisle. Zev followed. "Everything okay?"

I stayed silent.

"What's going on?" he asked, but I still refused to respond.

When we made it up a few rows, Zev popped open the over-head bin where my guitar was waiting. He reached in to get it.

"I can do it myself," I fumed.

I stood on my tippy toes and tried to get Ruby out. I was having a hard time maneuvering with my backpack and all the people around me.

"I got it," Zev said.

"No." I didn't need him and his stupid height.

"Sari, why are you being like this?" he asked.

I tugged at Ruby until she was free, and then I just turned and walked toward the front of the plane. It wasn't the most elegant exit—the pathway wasn't that wide and my case kept clunking into each row of seats as I passed—but Zev got the point. Anything I had said earlier on the flight no longer held true.

We got held up near the end as another passenger was trying to get something out of a bin. Zev put his hand on my shoulder and I shook it off.

"Tell me what I did, so I can fix it," he pleaded.

There was no fixing this.

I turned to face him. "You know what you did. Look, we have to get through this car ride, so I will pretend everything is fine." My voice was a harsh whisper. "I'm not going to make things weird for Fitz and his friend." I didn't even know the guy's name, I wasn't about to make him regret doing me a favor. "But you need to leave me alone. I can't take you right now."

"Just tell me, what did I do?"

"Stop."

"Sari, what—"

"Zev, please." My voice cracked. "Please just stop. Please."

He closed his eyes for a few seconds, but when he reopened them, he didn't say anything. We made it off the plane, and I saw Fitz standing with a group of people waiting for their bags.

"Hey," he said putting out both of his fists—one for me to bump, one for Zev. "Hanging in there?"

He was directing the question to Zev because of his meltdown before takeoff, but I was the one who was freaking out now. However, I was doing my best to contain the hurt and rage, so no one would notice.

"I'll meet you guys at baggage claim," I said, forcing a smile. They both checked things right before boarding that they needed to pick up gate side. I didn't. Mine would be coming the more traditional route. It gave me the perfect excuse to get away from everyone for a moment without causing a scene.

"Catch ya there," Fitz said.

Zev stayed quiet.

Now if he'd only do that for the next several hours, I could get home and never have to deal with him again.

TWENTY-EIGHT

I meant to race to baggage claim so I could have one less run-in with Zev, but my heels made that impossible. I was moving slower than any of the people I came across at Gram's retirement community. I wanted to take the shoes off, but the floor of the main concourse was beyond gross. People were tracking dirt and water in from outside. It was raining pretty hard here.

I dodged suitcases on wheels and travelers running to catch planes. The shoes were crushing my feet, it was like they had a death grip on me. The only thing that felt worse was the pain in my heart from Zev's lies.

Three and half hours, I'd be back home. I just needed to keep reminding myself. Somehow I made it down to the luggage carousel. I wedged my way between a woman in a leopard print jacket and a man who might have actually taken a bath in cologne. The musky scent tickled my nose, but I wasn't moving. The spot was right where the bags dropped out. Not only did I want to find mine as soon as possible, but I also wanted to avoid any unnecessary steps. I was never wearing heels again.

On the upside, it took me so long to get to baggage claim that I didn't have to wait more than a couple of minutes for the rumble of the conveyer belt to come on, and the first suitcases to make the rounds. On the downside, it also wasn't long until my travel companions were at my side.

"Found ya," Fitz said.

Just great.

Zev was behind him, but he was staring at the ground. Maybe, by a small miracle, I had managed to get through to him. Or maybe he finally realized that lying to someone you said you love is a completely rotten thing to do and doesn't deserve any understanding or kindness.

A large black suitcase with a silver ribbon fell out of the shoot. The ribbon was my dad's idea. He really loved playing off our last name, and it was just easier to humor him. "That's me," I said, reaching for the bag. Fitz grabbed it for me, lifting it like it was empty instead of stuffed with a week's worth of clothing, books, and other supplies.

"Thanks," I said, genuinely impressed. "Is it okay if I wait for you by the door?"

I didn't want to be rude by leaving him there, but I couldn't stand being near Zev a second longer than I had to.

Fitz didn't care.

"Any word from your friend?" I asked, as I lifted the handle to the suitcase and balanced Ruby against it.

"Yeah. Dylan's been circling around. He should be out front in a few minutes."

Dylan. That was his name. "Great." I pointed to the door to the left. "I'll be right over there."

I bit my lip at the view out the window. Trees were shaking, branches were whipping around, and the rain was coming down. This was the worst I had seen it in ages, and if the forecasters were right, this was just the beginning. The storm was supposed to be moving toward Boston from New York, which meant we'd be driving right into the heart of it.

I pulled out my umbrella, although I wasn't sure it was going to hold up long against those winds. Gram had wanted me to take her rain poncho, and I should have listened. I figured I'd just be running to a car; how wet could I get? Ha. I'd be drenched in a matter of seconds. I pulled my phone from the pocket of my backpack. If I didn't want it to get ruined, I'd have to wrap it in my T-shirt and then put it away.

Shoot. I never wrote my mom back. I had a gazillion messages waiting. This was Zev's fault. He distracted me. Right as I was about to respond, He-Who-Must-Not-Be-Named and Fitz walked over.

"Dylan's right outside," Fitz said. "Ready?"

I nodded. My mom waited this long, she could wait a few more minutes, I'd text her in the car. I just wanted to get on the road. I put the phone away and followed the guys toward the exit. I was finally leaving the airport!

There was a mixture of relief and fear as the automatic doors to my escape opened. Relief that I was one step closer to home, fear because Mother Nature seemed to resent my homecoming. Wind smacked me in the face, sending my hair flying in every direction, and even though we were still under an awning, we were getting sprayed with rain. It wasn't incredibly heavy yet, but the gusts were sending it everywhere. I opened the umbrella, but it didn't stop the water that was being blown at my body.

"That's Dylan's car," Fitz yelled, pointing to a car about ten feet away on the other side of the street. "Run for it?"

I nodded, and I gave it my best attempt, but with an umbrella, backpack, guitar, giant rolling suitcase, and heels from hell, it was more like a turtle-paced jog.

"Let me help you," Zev said, staying by my side.

"No." I'd rather have been blown away to Oz than take another favor from him.

Fitz made it to the car and looked back at us. Before I knew it, he jogged over and took my suitcase and Ruby. "Let me," he said.

I didn't object. He made it back to the car a second time before I even got there once.

He was waiting under an awning outside the car with a guy, who had to be Dylan, when Zev and I finally approached.

"Sari," I said, introducing myself.

"Dylan." Whoa, Fitz's friend was just as hot as Fitz. He was about five foot ten, Asian, beautiful brown eyes, amazing cheekbones, really warm smile, and killer abs which I totally tried not to stare at even though his T-shirt was plastered against them due to the rain. Well, if I had to be stuck in a car with my ex, at least there were two hot guys coming along, too.

"And I'm Zev."

I very maturely did not throw in that his alias was the lying, cheating lowlife of New York City or Voldemort or Lucifer or whatever else I could come up with. Instead I just said, "Thank you so much for taking us. You don't know how much this—"

Dylan interrupted me. "Definitely want to hear more about you guys, but why don't we do it once we're all packed up and in the car?"

"Smart thinking," I said.

"All this is yours?" Dylan asked, surveying our luggage. "I

didn't realize there'd be so much. Might be a tight fit. Let's see what we can do."

Tight fit was an understatement. Dylan's car was a little sedan, and his trunk was filled with stuff he was bringing back to school. I held the umbrella over the trunk as we tried to maneuver, but I was just getting in the way, so I shut it. Instead, we just tried to load the car as fast as possible.

We took out one of Dylan's boxes and managed to get all the carry-ons and Fitz's suitcase in the trunk, but that still left the box, my giant suitcase, guitar and Zev's duffel—which wasn't exactly minuscule, either. "Sorry, these are going to have to go in the back with you," Dylan told Zev and me.

"That's fine," I said. "We can put them in between us." That was even preferable, it was like my own little gate keeping Zev away from me.

Fitz and Dylan tried to maneuver my suitcase into the middle seat, but it just about hit the ceiling of the car, blocking vision to the rear window. Fitz pulled it out of the backseat. "I think one of you is going to have to sit in the middle, so we can put this on the floor in the back." When I was a kid I loved that elevated middle floor section. I thought of it as a little footrest, but now it meant I'd have to sit next to Zev again.

Fitz put the suitcase on the floor behind the passenger's side, put the box on the seat and then piled the duffel on top. The guitar was going to go half on that, half on my lap. "Think you guys will be okay?"

"Yeah." We would have to be. I needed to get back to New York. I squeezed into the middle seat, and even though Zev was super skinny, we barely fit with all the stuff. He angled himself so he was almost sitting on his hip, and he was squished up against me. It was so tight, that Dylan had to push the door closed.

"Put your seat belt on," I told Zev after he wiped the rain off his glasses. I still hated him, but I didn't want him dead, and we were about to drive in a storm. "Watch it," I said, as his hand hit my butt.

"You were the one who told me to put on my seat belt," he said. "I'm trying to get to the buckle." I lifted myself up so he could reach. "Don't forget yours," he said.

This time I had to reach under him. "See, I'm not complaining." He gave me a weak smile, like he was trying to be endearing or get on my good side. I did not smile back.

"Everyone all right back there?" Dylan asked.

"Mm-hmm," I answered.

But "all right" was a relative notion. I'd never truly be all right after what Zev did to me, but I'd survive, even trapped with him in an uncomfortable car. I literally had no wiggle room. I couldn't move. The box was jammed up against me on one side and Zev on the other. He was so close, I could feel his breath on my neck. But there was nowhere to turn. If I shifted so that the back of my head was toward him, my face would be millimeters from his duffel and my guitar case. That was even worse. I'd just have to deal with his hot air. I raised my hand to my neck, to try and block it, but it didn't work. The constant reminder of Zev was still there. I let out a deep breath.

This was going to be a very long ride.

TWENTY-NINE

Fifteen minutes in the car already felt like fifteen hours. There was no way to pretend Zev wasn't there when he was practically on top of me, but I was doing the best I could to zone him out. At least he wasn't talking much, he just sat there sulking while I exchanged pleasantries with Dylan. I shared the abbreviated (and edited to leave out any mention of Zev) version of my story: high school senior, aspiring singer with a can't-miss performance tomorrow. In return, I got full name, Dylan Chen, senior at NYU with a journalism concentration, internship at GroupIt and hoping for a full-time job after graduation.

"That's really cool," I said, leaning forward, bringing myself closer to the guys up front and farther away from Zev. "Is that why you're in a rush to get back? Work?"

"No, girlfriend," he answered. "Her birthday is tomorrow, and no way I'm missing it. I have a whole night planned."

"That's great," I said, giving Zev the side eye. "I love hearing about a guy who goes out of his way for his girlfriend, a guy who she can count on. Doesn't happen all the time."

Sure, I was being passive-aggressive, but I didn't care. Zev hurt me, and it wasn't like I could blow up on him in front of everyone, so I'd have to make do with a few subtle digs.

"Yeah, well," Dylan said, "I owe her, and I'd do anything for Gina."

Fitz laughed. "Except get her a Christmas gift."

I was missing something. "Huh?"

"Part of the reason I can*not* miss tomorrow is that I royally messed up Christmas," Dylan said. "Although it wasn't entirely my fault. We were in separate cities for winter break. I was in Boston, she was in Dallas. I called her, sent her a funny e-card, how was I supposed to know to send a gift?"

He caught my eye in the rearview mirror, and I shook my head at him. "Because it was Christmas! And she's your girlfriend."

"I know, I know."

"Wait until you hear what she sent him," Fitz said.

"An iWatch," Dylan said.

"Oooh, and you got her nothing?" I asked. "Not even when you got back to school, not even a real card?" I didn't want to make him feel bad, but he was right, he had screwed up. Not nearly as bad as Zev, but still. . . .

"I thought it was too late. Christmas was over," he said.

"I don't think anything's ever too late," Zev said, joining the conversation.

I rolled my eyes, then I tugged at my seat belt to get more slack and leaned farther forward. I'd try to wedge Zev out of this discussion as best I could.

"So what are you doing for Gina's birthday?" I asked.

"I'm going all out," he said. "If I screw this up, she will kill me. I told her to expect something epic, so I am throwing her a huge surprise party. That box next to you," he said. "It's decorations. There are collages of us and her and her friends that I put together, little twinkly lights, and way too many balloons. Hopefully enough to make her forget Christmas. I got a whole room at a bar near school. Her roommates are going to decorate while I take her to her favorite restaurant. By the time we make it to the party everyone should be there. And I ordered her the most over-the-top chocolate cake from Andrea's Bakery."

"That place is my favorite," I said.

"Hers, too."

"It sounds perfect," I told him.

"I hope so," he said.

Fitz slapped Dylan's shoulder. "He's been planning it for ages. It's going to be the party of the year."

Those words made my skin crawl. The last "party of the year" practically destroyed me. Still, I couldn't help but smile at the bromance Fitz and Dylan seemed to have going on.

"What about you two?" I asked. "How did you guys become friends?"

"Actually," Dylan said, "My ex-girlfriend was Fitz's RA his freshman year."

"RA?" I asked.

"Resident assistant. An upperclassman who lives and helps out in the halls," he said.

Right, I knew that. They got free housing, too. I definitely wanted to try for that myself when the time came.

"I was in their hall all the time," Dylan went on, "practically lived there. Fitz and I started hanging out."

"We're still going strong," Fritz added. "The friendship lasted longer than the relationship."

"She was a senior, I was a sophomore," Dylan said. "As it got closer to her graduation, we kind of realized a future would be hard. She was going to be in L.A., I was still going to be in school. So we ended things."

I nodded, forcing myself not to glance at Zev. "I think it's a good idea, ending things before graduation. Start the next chapter fresh, don't have to worry about anything holding you back."

"I don't agree," Zev said.

Do not look at him, I instructed myself. *Act like you didn't even hear him.*

"I think if you want it to work, you make it work," he went on. "You don't just throw something out, you figure it out."

Just great. Now he was the one trying to talk in code.

I was not biting. I refused to acknowledge him, but unfortunately Dylan did.

"I agree, man. Gina and I are staying together. No way I'm letting her go."

I shifted in my seat. I was not going to sit there and have a conversation about couples needing to fight for their love. I had to change the subject. "Tell us what to expect as college freshmen," I said, picking a topic I figured Dylan and Fitz would be able to drone on about for hours.

I was right. The two went on and on about coed bathrooms, roommates, picking classes by schedule and professor, and so on. As they talked, I stared out the window. The rain was coming down even harder now. Dylan had the windshield wipers on full speed, but they didn't seem to be doing anything.

We passed by a tow truck and two cars pulled over by the

side of the road. Or at least that's what I think it was, it was hard to see clearly through the downpour.

There was thunder and flashes of lightning. I jumped when a branch hit the front window. We all did.

"Didn't expect that," Dylan said, and the conversation about college petered out as he became hyperfocused on the road. He was going even slower than before and his hands were gripping the steering wheel so tightly that his knuckles were white. I sat back in my seat and made sure my seat belt was secure.

"I've never seen it this bad," Dylan said, more to himself than to any of us. It wasn't very reassuring.

After that none of us said a word, letting Dylan concentrate on driving instead.

The car had an eerie feeling to it. None of us were talking, but it wasn't silent. The rain was smacking down on the car, the tires were swishing through the water on the road, and there seemed to be a slight crackle all around us. The air felt thick, like I was underwater. Only there was no coming up for oxygen. The lack of conversation was giving me too much time to think. I didn't know where to focus, not with Zev plastered to my side, his body warm against mine. There weren't many options, so I kept my eyes glued straight ahead, looking out the front window.

It had gotten dark out. I couldn't see anything. I prayed Dylan had a better vantage point from the front seat.

A flash of lightning streaked through the sky followed by a large boom. Then another. The thunder was getting louder.

Just God bowling, I told myself. That explanation worked when I was little, but it wasn't having quite the same effect now.

I wasn't going to say it, but I was getting scared. I couldn't even make out if there were other cars on the highway.

Another loud, violent crack rumbled through the sky. My whole body quivered, and I wanted to reach out and grab Zev's knee, but I stopped myself. He was a cheating jerk-face, and I was not going to touch any part of him that I didn't have to.

I'd just text Trina. That was it. She'd help me keep it together. I moved Ruby aside, to reach my backpack, and then I realized it—my backpack, my phone—they weren't there. They were in the trunk.

THIS DAY SUCKED!

I readjusted my guitar, sat back, and closed my eyes. I wasn't going to sleep, not with all the thunder. Instead, I decided to count the seconds between the rumbles from the sky. It wound up not having quite the calming effect I had hoped for, so I gave up. I just sat there, silently, wishing for this trip to end.

Zev eventually broke the quiet.

"Sari," he said softly. "It's your mom. She wants you to text her back. She says she's left you dozens of messages."

Crap, crap, crap, crap, crap.

I never got back to her; I had totally forgotten.

I hated doing this, but I had no choice. "Can I use your phone for a minute?" I asked him.

Zev handed it over.

> Mom, it's Sari. I'm sorry. My phone is in my bag. I'm fine. We're still on the road. Should be home in a couple of hours. Please stop texting Zev.

She didn't like my response.

> **MRS. SILVER**
> I need to know what's going on, Sari. If you don't have your phone, then I have no choice but to text him.

> Mom! Please don't.

> **MRS. SILVER**
> Sari, I am worried. I need to know what is going on.

This was getting me nowhere. "Guys, I'm sorry," I said to the two up front, "I just need to make a quick call. Is that okay?"

"Sure," they said.

I dialed my mother. She picked up on the first ring, "Sari, is that you?"

"Yes, Mom, it's me. Everything's okay. I'll be home soon. I'm sorry I didn't call earlier."

There was a pause, but surprisingly she didn't yell at me for my lack of communication. "Where are you?" she asked instead.

"Somewhere in Connecticut."

"Sari," she said, the concern coming through her voice, "that's where the brunt of the storm is right now. You really shouldn't be on the road."

"I told you everything is fine. Let's talk when I get home."

"I need to know that you are okay. I want updates," she said.

I really needed her to back off, just this once. "I *am* okay, and I told you my phone is in the trunk."

"Then I'll text Zev."

I couldn't deal. Did she have to be like this *today*? "Please don't."

"Sari, if I can't get through to you, I don't have a choice."

She wasn't hearing me. I felt the heat rising through my body. How could she not tell how desperate I was for her to just to drop this? "*Please*. No. I'm begging you."

"You are my daughter," she said, "and you are out in the middle of a storm."

"Mom, I know." I struggled not to yell. "But you are *not* listening to me. I'm fine." My free hand was digging into the leather seat so hard, I had to force myself to stop before I made five fingernail-size holes and owed Dylan new upholstery.

"I just want to make sure of that," she said, disregarding everything I just told her. "I'm not going to sit here and worry myself into a panic just because you and Zev had a little tiff."

"It was not just a *tiff*, Mom," I seethed. "I can't talk about it now. I'm in the car. *With people*."

"Well," she said. "If you hadn't been avoiding me all day then you wouldn't have to talk now, now would you?"

Was she seriously doing this to me? I was so at a loss that I didn't even respond.

"Zev answers me," she went on, like nothing I said meant anything. "He's been lovely all day, and unless you can give me a good reason not to, I'm going to keep texting him for updates. I don't understand what the big deal is."

The big deal? *The big deal?!* "WELL, MAYBE, I DON'T LIKE MY MOTHER BEING ALL CHATTY WITH MY CHEATING EX-BOYFRIEND."

Everything got silent. My mom. Me. I couldn't even hear the

rain anymore, but that was probably because my heart was beating so loudly.

Oh no. What a fool.

Did I really just scream that in front of everyone? Here I was purposefully not talking about the breakup, and then I go and yell it at the top of my lungs in a car full of people. What was wrong with me?

"Your what?" my mom asked gently.

"My *cheating* ex," I said, my voice quieter, but shaking. At this point it didn't matter if Fitz and Dylan heard everything, they already got the humiliating headline. "I caught your perfect Zev kissing someone else. Still need to talk to him?"

"Oh, sweetie, I'm so sorry," she said. "Why didn't you tell me?"

I choked back tears. I was not going to cry. "I didn't want to think about it. Mom, I'm in the car. I'll talk to you later, okay?" My breathing was shallow, and my heart was racing. I just needed to get off the phone. And maybe a vanishing spell or an invisibility cloak.

"But what happened?" she pressed. "Are you okay? How are—"

"MOM! I'm in the *car*." I was not going to have this conversation with her in front of Zev.

"I'm just worried about you."

"I know. But how many times do I have to say I can't do this now?"

"Okay, okay. And Sari?"

"What?" I was a hair away from losing it again.

"I love you."

"I love you, too."

We hung up, and I handed the phone back to Zev.

I had *really* not meant to blurt that out in the car. It felt so real now. Zev and I were over. Done. It shouldn't matter that people knew, but it felt weird. My head was spinning. And the others . . .

The tension in the car was palpable. This was all my doing. I was so embarrassed. So much for not causing a scene. I couldn't even make it to New York without losing it. *Great job, Sari.* Now, I'd made things horrible for everyone.

As each second ticked away, I felt like I was suffocating in the silence. Should I say something? Should I explain? Apologize? Promise them they'll never have to deal with me again after today? I needed to do something.

Dylan beat me to it.

"Dude, not cool," he said to Zev.

"Yeah, man," Fitz agreed.

"It wasn't like . . . ," Zev started, but then just gave up. The look of warning Fitz was shooting him may have had something to do with it. Zev rested his head against the window and kept his focus outside.

I hoped he stayed that way.

Fitz twisted back to face me. He was about to say something, but then his eyes got wide and his attention snapped back to the front.

The car was spinning.

"Hold on!" Dylan called out.

He'd lost control. My feet pressed into the floor, my whole body clenched, and without even realizing it, I grabbed Zev's arm.

This could be it. My mind raced. Zev. My family. My

performance. I shouldn't have yelled at my mom. She warned me to stay in Florida, I should have listened. I didn't want to die. I didn't want Zev to die. Love, hate, fear, anger, and sadness—I felt it all. This was not supposed to be the end.

There was a loud prolonged screech, as we headed straight for the side of the road.

I was too stunned to scream.

I was jerked forward and back, and then we crashed into the guardrail.

THIRTY

"We're okay, we're okay," Zev whispered into my hair. His arms were wrapped around me, and my head was on his chest. "I got you. We're fine. I love you, Sari."

He had pulled me toward him as we swerved, and I had let him.

"How are you guys in front?" Zev asked.

"Okay," Dylan answered. Fitz nodded in agreement.

I sat back up. I wasn't hurt. I was alive. We all were. Thank God.

My breathing was loud and heavy, I couldn't get it under control. I couldn't calm down. I pushed Zev's arm away from me and rocked myself back and forth.

"How are you guys?" Dylan asked.

"Fine," I said. And then I broke down into tears.

I don't know why. I wasn't in pain, but I couldn't stop.

"You're all right," Zev said, and kissed the top of my head. I pulled away, still sobbing.

I knew that, I knew I was all right. But it was just everything. The stress, the airport, the flight, the cheating, the heartbreak. I was overtired and upset, and the whole day just came pouring out of me.

"Sari?" Fitz asked.

"I'm fine," I said louder than I intended and began crying harder.

Dylan got out to check the car. I needed out, too. I needed air.

"Move, *please*," I told Zev. "I have to get out."

"It's pouring," he said. "It was just a light bump. We're safer in here."

"Zev, I need to get out of this car."

"Sari, with the traffic, we're better off in here."

I started banging my fists into his arm. "I don't care. I want out. Let me out."

"Okay, okay," he said, and opened the door.

The rain slammed into me, I was drenched in seconds, but I could *not* get back in that car next to Zev. I moved toward the trunk and leaned against it, the rain mixing with my tears.

Zev followed. "Sari."

"Go away, Zev."

He put out his hand. "Come on."

"Please, just leave me alone." The sound of rain smacking pavement muffled my voice, but he heard me. He finally shook his head and got back inside the car.

I felt hollow. I leaned my head back, the rain rushing down, and screamed into the sky, my body convulsing in sobs.

"Hey, you're going to be okay." A pair of arms wrapped around me. It wasn't Zev, it was Fitz. I let myself crumple into him. We just stood there like that in the storm until my blubbering passed. He didn't say anything, he just squeezed me tight, letting me cry it out.

"I'm sorry," I said, pulling away.

"Nothing to be sorry about. Take the front. I'll sit in the back with him."

"Really?" I didn't know what to say. Fitz just kept doing all these amazingly nice things for me. Buying me a smoothie when he thought I needed one, getting me a ride to New York, and now this. I didn't deserve it, but I was grateful for it.

"Yeah," he said.

"Thank you."

I walked around to the front passenger side and got in. I was a soggy mess. I pulled down the sun visor and checked myself in the mirror. All the makeup I had so carefully applied earlier this morning ran in streaks down my face. I looked worse than the sole survivor in a horror movie—the one who fought off dozens of zombies through a muddy swamp but somehow managed to prevail. That's what I was going to have to do—prevail.

"Here," Dylan said, handing me a tissue. "I'm so sorry, you guys. I just lost control. The car was hydroplaning, and I couldn't do anything to stop it. The car's okay. I only grazed the rail. We should be fine. Are you fine?"

I wasn't the only one spiraling out. Dylan seemed pretty shaken.

"I should never have told you guys to hang on," he babbled on. "You know I read the best thing in situations like that is to stay loose. It's why so many babies and drunk people survive accidents, they don't stiffen up, they're limber during impact."

Fitz leaned over and put his hands on Dylan's shoulders.

"It's not your fault. Take a breath. You did a good job. We're all okay."

"Yeah," I said, pulling myself together for him. "You did everything right. You got us out of this safely. The roads are a mess; it wasn't you."

The tension in his muscles seemed to relax.

Fitz grabbed his phone and showed the screen to Dylan. "I looked up some hotels. There's one right off that exit over there. Let's stay there tonight." He called up the directions. "See, it's not even a mile. We'll get back on the road in the morning when this is over. You'll still make it to Gina with a ton of time."

Dylan didn't respond.

"Hey," Fitz said, squeezing his friend's shoulder. "She'd rather you get there tomorrow and be safe."

Dylan nodded.

I took a deep breath as my hands clenched around the tissue. Everything Fitz said made sense. I knew that. There was no arguing it. We could barely see the road in front of us. We'd already had a minor accident, and the weather was only getting worse. It wasn't safe to continue, but I just wanted to get home.

I felt like I really was in a horror movie, stuck on a trip that would never end.

I buckled up, because I had no idea what I was in store for next.

THIRTY-ONE

"Dude, this looks like a really nice hotel," Dylan said, when we pulled into the parking lot. "What are the prices like?"

Fitz shook his head. "Didn't look. Guess we're about to find out."

Not that it really mattered. It wasn't like we could pick up and go somewhere else, the whole point was to get off the road as fast as possible. Making it to this place had been scary enough.

"Let's get our stuff," he said.

"My umbrella's back there if you want it," I told Fitz. I was already sopping, at this point I didn't care if I used it or not.

"I don't think it will do much good. More trouble trying to keep it open. Let's just try to get everything inside as fast as we can."

I opened my door and slammed it shut quickly, and then opened the backside passenger door and grabbed Ruby. Fitz came over and helped me move Zev's duffel and get my suitcase out. "I got it," he said. "Just grab your backpack."

Dylan passed it to me, and I started to run, heels and all. Wearing the shoes still felt like I was walking on hot coals, but they were pretty much glued to my feet at this point. I made it inside and rushed to the check-in desk, the others right beside me.

"Please tell me you have some rooms," I said, rocking side to side, trying to momentarily relieve the pressure off each foot.

"You're in luck, we do," the chipper guy at the desk said. He didn't comment about our appearance or the weather, he just tapped away on his computer.

"Thank God," I said.

"How many do you need?" he asked.

I turned to the guys.

"Two?" Fitz said, "you can have one and the rest of us can share?"

Dylan nodded and Zev shrugged.

"Two," I told the guy.

"Okay," he said and punched some more keys. "That will be $453.10 total, including tax."

"*How* much?!" I asked. I couldn't afford half of that on my own. I couldn't even afford it if we split it four ways. Especially since I wanted to give Dylan some gas money, too. "Hang on," I told him.

I turned back to my travel party.

"What do you want to do?" Fitz asked.

He was leaving the decision up to me. Part of me just wanted to go back to the car for the night, while the other part wanted to say screw it and use my emergency credit card to get a room of my own. Practicality won out. Sleeping outside wasn't really an option, and I couldn't justify spending that kind of money, not when things were tight like they were. And it wasn't like I was staying with three guys I was unsure about. Plus, Zev was there. While I hated him and didn't trust him when it came to my heart or our relationship, I did when it came to everything else. "I guess we can all split one room. It makes the most sense."

I turned back to the desk clerk and told him what we wanted. Well, not *wanted*, but needed. Behind me, Dylan said something about being hungry and how we should look for some food. Zev and Fitz agreed, but I refused to be a part of any conversation where Zev was involved. Even though I was starving.

Instead I made myself focus on taking in the lobby. It was pretty. Large crystal chandeliers, marble floors, leather couches, sleek design. Classy with a modern touch. Wasn't how I expected to share my first hotel room with Zev. A couple of my friends had been talking about getting rooms for after prom. That seemed like a lifetime ago, though. Things had changed so much since then. Before it seemed exciting, thrilling, grown-up. Not like *this*.

The desk clerk finally finished and handed me the key cards. I took mine and handed the other three to Dylan. I didn't want to risk my fingers brushing against Zev's. I took my suitcase and headed to the elevator, leaving a trail of water behind me. I got on first and pressed the number *six* and waited in silence as the others filed in. I watched the floor numbers light up as we got higher, keeping my attention there instead of on my pain—both the emotional and the physical.

The door opened, and I led the way to our room. Once inside, I claimed the bed closest to the door. Fitz sat on the other one and Dylan threw his stuff next to him.

"Your girlfriend's gonna be jealous," Fitz told him.

Dylan snorted. "Of you or me?"

"You, definitely you," Fitz answered.

They were laughing, but I saw nothing funny about this situation. I was still stuck with my ex. Dylan and Fitz might have been willing to share a bed, but I was not going to do the same with Zev, who was just standing there in the middle of the room, probably trying to figure out what to do. I was going to make that one easy for him.

"That's you." I pointed to the little sofa in front of the TV on the other side of the room from me by the window.

It was way too small for him, but he was going to have to deal. I'd been dealing with uncomfortable annoyances all day. He could suck it up.

"Anyone need the bathroom?" I asked.

After they all shook their heads no, I yanked off my shoes, grabbed my backpack and guitar, went to my newly appointed studio, and locked the door.

"Did she just take her guitar to the bathroom?" I heard Dylan ask.

"Whatever, man," Fitz answered, "I'm not questioning it. I don't want to see her cry again."

They must have thought I was a complete mess.

The worst part is they weren't wrong. Even now I was fighting tears.

Dropping my stuff on the ground and letting the cool tile soothe my aching feet, I leaned against the counter and stared at myself in the mirror. My eyes were red and puffy *again*, I had makeup streaks *again*, and I basically looked downright miserable *again*. It was the theme of my week, and it needed to end now. I had a performance tomorrow night, and I had to be at the top of my game.

I turned on the shower, let it get nice and hot, and got inside.

The steady stream of water beating down my back felt relaxing. I lathered the shampoo in my hair and breathed in the lemon and sage scent. This was what I needed—to wash away the day, the week, and the memories of Zev.

A *clean* start, as my father would probably say.

I watched the suds and the water circle down the drain.

It was time to move forward.

THIRTY-TWO

I was planning on making the bathroom my own little studio and practice my set, but I was going to have to wait a little bit. The steam was so dense, I could barely see my own hand, and I didn't want to take Ruby out of her case yet.

Instead I brushed my hair, and did some vocal warm-ups.

It was nice having a minute to myself, letting the rest of the world melt away.

But my moment of peace didn't last long.

There was a knock on the door. "Sari?" Zev said.

Of course, it was him.

Why couldn't he leave me alone? I couldn't open the door even if I wanted to, I wasn't dressed and the towel didn't quite make it all the way around. It was okay on top, but there was a slight gap by my hips that revealed way too much. "What?" I snapped.

"Your mom's texting again."

I closed my eyes and shook my head.

I couldn't believe she was still contacting him. Yes, I should have called her once we got to the hotel, but *she* didn't know we stopped somewhere. As far as she was concerned we were still on the road, which meant even though she knew what happened with Zev, and how much it bothered me, it wasn't enough to stop her from texting him. "I'll take care of it," I said.

I looked at my dress on the floor. It used to be my favorite. I was going to wear it tomorrow night. Not anymore, not even if it magically got perfectly pressed. It no longer felt lucky the way it used to. But for now, it looked like I was stuck putting it back on. It was that or smoothie-covered sweats, because I was going to have to leave the bathroom at some point, and no way I was asking Fitz or Dylan to go through my suitcase with all my dirty underwear and ask them to find me something else to wear. And I certainly wasn't asking Zev for any help.

I put on the dress, spread a towel on the floor and sat down.

I grabbed my phone from my backpack. Holy crap, I had a lot of messages.

Stay calm, I reminded myself as I called my mom. I did not want to get myself worked up again. I needed to stay composed. I needed to unwind and prepare for my show, not get agitated.

"Sari, you got your phone back," she said after she picked up.

Uh-uh, she wasn't getting out of this *that* easy. "You said you wouldn't text Zev anymore," I reminded her.

"I didn't." There was a pause.

"He told me, Mom," I said, rather even temperedly, if I do say so myself.

"It was your father."

Really? *Really?* She was trying for a technicality? Wow. I guess next time they told me to be home by nine, I could just pretend I thought they meant 9:00 a.m. "Seriously, Mom? You knew what I meant."

"Sari, we were worried. Audrey was saying how bad it is in Connecticut right now. She was wearing that hot-pink dress we love, by the way, but to my point, there were reports of accidents, and Dad and I got scared. We just wanted to make sure you were all right."

I decided not to argue or tell her I had no idea what dress she was talking about, but I was definitely using this next time I needed a get-out-of-jail-free card. "I'm okay. We pulled over, and checked into a hotel. We just got here," I threw in quickly, before she lambasted me for not telling her earlier. "The roads were bad, so we decided we'd leave for New York when it clears up tomorrow." I left out the part about the accident. She was already paranoid enough about this trip, I didn't need to give proof to her fears.

Not that that kept her from worrying about the other aspects of my travel adventure.

"You're staying in a hotel room with three guys?" she asked. "Sari, I don't like this."

"You didn't like me on the road, either." I really couldn't win with her.

I could imagine her frowning and the crease in her forehead as she furrowed her brow at my words.

"Why didn't you get your own room?" she asked.

"Because it was expensive."

"Sari, your safety is the most important thing. Your father and I will pay for it."

I bit my tongue to keep from pointing out that had she and my dad let me change to an earlier flight when I wanted to, it would have cost only two hundred dollars, which was less than my own hotel room, *and* I'd already be home by now. "Mom,

I'm safe. Honest. I'm not wasting the money on a hotel. It doesn't make sense."

"I'm not sure about this."

"Mom, it's already done." I did not want to have this conversation. I just wanted to be alone and play Ruby. Although, I wasn't really alone. I could hear the sound of the TV and murmur of voices coming from the hotel room. I had to remember to keep it down in here, I didn't need to air any more of my drama than I already had.

"Hold on," my mom said, "talk to your father."

I rolled my eyes as I heard her tell him about my rooming situation.

"Sari, sweetie," my dad said, getting on the line. "I don't like this."

Not him, too. "Want me to go check if the gift shop has some mace?" I asked. "I'll spray Zev if you want me to."

"I'm not joking here, Sari," he said. "This is not funny."

No kidding. "I know Dad. I just don't know what you guys want me to do." My voice was rising, and I brought it back down. "It's not safe to drive and the whole reason I didn't come home on Thursday was because of the money, getting my own room and spending more now makes this whole trip home a waste, and I can't do that. I need there to be a reason for it." After everything I'd been through, there had to be one upside to it all, even if it was just getting home in time for the show and saving a little cash.

"All right, just be careful," he said.

"I will."

"I love you, kiddo. Hold on, your brother wants to talk to you."

"No, I don't," I heard Dan grumble.

I knew the feeling. I wasn't in the mood to talk, either; I just wanted to play my guitar.

Dan got on the phone, anyway.

"Hi," he said.

"Hi."

"You alive?" he asked.

"Yup."

" 'K, stay that way."

"I'll try," I said, hesitantly. He was being too nice.

"Good," he told me, "because I'm taking your room when you go to college, and I can't do that if they turn it into a shrine."

There it was. We didn't have the biggest apartment in the world, and Dan and I both had makeshift rooms—basically my parents chopped up the living room and kitchen and put in fake walls. My room was a tiny bit bigger than Dan's. He knew I got upset when he said he was switching. I was very territorial when it came to my bedroom, which was basically like asking him to give me an extra hard time about it. Although, if I was being honest, I gave back just as good as I got.

But somehow, today, my little brother's crusty comment gave me my first real smile in a while. "I love you, too," I said.

"I know," he answered, but I knew he meant it. We may have had our fights, but he loved me and I loved him.

I might not have had a boyfriend anymore, but I had a kick-ass family—even if they pestered me *a lot*.

After I hung up, I finally took Ruby out of her case. It felt so good to have her back in my arms. I'd been waiting for this all day, but I didn't even manage to get my pick positioned between my fingers before there was another knock at the door.

"Sari?" It was Zev. Again.

Holy hell. I really couldn't take him. "I'm in *the bathroom*. Clearly I'm trying for some privacy."

"I just wanted to see if you wanted anything to eat. I'm going to go raid the vending machine, and check out the restaurant downstairs. Fitz said it has some decent options. Want anything?"

"What I want is to be left alone." I heard footsteps walk away from the door. Finally, he was taking the hint. A little too late.

My fingers were shaking with anger, I couldn't very well play like that. I carefully put Ruby back in her case.

Thanks to Zev and his talk about food, all I could think about was how hungry I was. I'd barely eaten anything all day. I reached into my bag and pulled out Gram's cookies. These would have to do, because there was no way I was taking anything from Zev, and I was *not* leaving this bathroom while he was still around.

After a couple of cookies, I still hadn't calmed down.

I called Trina. She always knew how to keep me from losing it.

"Where have you been?" she said, skipping the hello. "You haven't been picking up. I thought something happened."

"It almost did," I confessed.

"What?! Are you okay?"

I didn't know if it was the panic in her voice, the memory of what happened, or everything that was going on with Zev, but as I told her about spinning out of control and heading for the guardrail, I started crying again.

"Sari, tell me what I can do?" she said.

"Nothing, I'm fine." I hated being like this. I never considered myself a crier, and yet here I was continuing to let loose enough tears to fill an ocean. This week was the worst. "I just don't know how I'm going to get through the rest of this trip. I locked myself in the bathroom, so I didn't have to deal with you-know-who. But I'll have to see him eventually. And then I have another car ride with him. How am I supposed to breathe with him so close?"

"I'm coming to get you," she said.

"You can't. It's dangerous out there."

"Tomorrow morning. I'll pick you up. The storm will have passed here by then. Text me your address; I'll be there by ten a.m."

It was the sweetest offer, but I had to refuse. It was asking too much. "I'm still more than an hour out of the city. I can't make you do that."

"You're not *making* me do anything. I want to. Besides, I haven't seen my best friend all week, it will give us some time together."

I ripped apart another cookie. "Are you sure?"

"Absolutely."

I wasn't, though. "What about your mom and dad? It's one thing to drive a few blocks in the city, this is a big trip. They'll flip."

"You leave Gary and Sandy to me. You're not the only parent whisperer around here."

"Positive?" I asked, checking one more time.

"Positive."

I was already feeling a little better.

"Now that we've got that taken care of," she said. "Where's Ruby?"

"Right here."

"Good," she said, "now put me on speakerphone, and play me your set."

"What? No."

"I want to hear it," she insisted. "It will do us both some good. Music therapy."

Even though she couldn't see me, I nodded. I took Ruby back out and started to play.

It was a moment-to-moment struggle to keep myself from thinking of Zev, but he had already taken enough from me, I was not going to let him ruin my rehearsal time, too. *Focus on the music, Sari.*

I made myself concentrate on Ruby and the lyrics and the way the sound echoed in the bathroom. I kind of liked the acoustics. It was different. Before I knew it, I let myself go. I loved the feeling; time seemed to stand still. It felt like a couple of minutes, but that was impossible, I was already finishing my last song.

Trina started applauding.

"You are so ready for tomorrow!"

"You think?"

"I know," she said. "Now I'm going to hang up, and you're going to play the set again. You've got this, Sari. The music is going to help you get through this."

So was she. "Thank you for everything, Trina. I really don't know what I'd be doing without you. I hope you know, I'm always here for you, too. You're like a sister to me. One I got to choose."

"Same here, but let's stop before we start crying," she warned. "No sappy stuff, unless it's part of a song. I don't want you losing focus. Today and tomorrow are about the music, remember? Put the emotion there."

"Aye-aye, Captain."

We said good-bye, and I started playing again. This time it didn't take me any time to get in the zone. I wanted this sensation of getting lost in the music to last forever, or at least a little longer.

Only no such luck. There was another knock on the bathroom door.

THIRTY-THREE

"Zev! Go away! Enough already!" I shouted. How many times did I have to tell him?

"Uhh, Sari, this is Dylan."

Oh my God. I jumped up and opened the door. "Dylan, I'm so sorry."

"No worries. I didn't want to bother you, but I really have to use the bathroom. Sorry. I'll only be a minute."

"Don't apologize. It's all yours," I said, picking up my stuff. "I'm done."

I couldn't believe I had been so rude. Other than when we first got to the hotel, I hadn't even thought about if someone else needed the bathroom or wanted to shower. We'd been traveling all day; of course they'd want to get in here at some point, but I was hogging it. They were probably too afraid to say anything. Afraid I'd snap. And I did.

"Coast is clear," Fitz said, when I emerged from my island of seclusion.

"Huh?"

"Zev. He went down to the lobby to make some calls."

Right, because that's what courteous people did. They excused themselves when they wanted some privacy, they didn't steal the common area.

Fitz was lying down on his bed, flicking channels on the TV.

"I'm sorry about taking so long in there." I put my stuff next to my bed, and fell backward onto it. "I can't believe I yelled at Dylan."

"No big deal. Trust me, it takes a lot more to faze him."

"True," Dylan said, reentering the room and grabbing the remote from Fitz. "The bathroom is all yours again if you want it."

"That's okay, but thank you." I did want to keep playing, but I had overstepped enough today. "You both have been really great. Sorry for adding so much drama to your trip."

"Made it more interesting," Dylan answered. Although I highly doubted that was the case.

"And stop apologizing," Fitz said, swiping the remote back. "Not your fault. We've all had days like this. Are you okay?"

That was nice of him to say, but I felt like I should be begging their forgiveness for having to deal with Zev and me. "Yeah, thanks," I said, sitting back up. Fitz was looking at me. It was like he was trying to figure out if I was lying—which I was. "Much better." The music helped, but I was still a mess. But I didn't want them to feel obligated to try and cheer me up, so I tried to put on my best happy face. It wasn't their job to make me feel better. They had a rough day, too. They deserved a break without me being a bigger imposition than I'd already been.

I told them about Trina picking me up tomorrow.

"Sari, I can sit in the back with Zev," Fitz said. "You won't have to talk to him; Dylan and I can be your buffer."

"Thanks, but Trina was looking for an excuse to drive on the highway, anyway," I lied again. "She'll be pissed at me if I don't let her come."

"Well, we won't leave until we're sure she gets here," Dylan said. "Just in case."

"Thanks." But I knew I could count on Trina.

"And I don't know if you're going to want to hear this or not," Dylan added, pointing toward the microwave in the corner of the room, "but Zev brought you some stuff."

Sitting on top of the microwave were peanut butter M&M'S, Oreos, and one of those cups of macaroni and cheese that you just add water to and heat. My top three go-to stress snacks. I practically lived on them during finals last semester. Zev was a Twizzler and gummy bears guy, so there was no doubt they were intended for me. I didn't understand him. Why was he trying so hard? Why did he care? Was he just messing with me? Was he really sorry? Tons of questions swirled around my head, but I couldn't think about them. I had to push them aside. No more Zev thoughts until after my show.

"You guys can have them," I said. "I'm just going to get some sleep; I'm pretty tired."

"Want us to turn off the TV?" Fitz asked.

I shook my head. It wouldn't matter. I was exhausted. I barely slept last night, and with everything that happened today, I was worn out. I was sure I could sleep through anything. I crawled under the covers, not even bothering to change out of the dress.

I was just ready to crash and for this day to be over.

THIRTY-FOUR

A snore, a really *loud* snore woke me from my sleep. I couldn't tell if it was Fitz or Dylan, but one of them had some major nasal issues. They could give the tuba section in my school band a serious run for its money.

I glanced at the clock on the nightstand separating the two beds. I had only been asleep for three hours.

No!

It was so not to time to be up. I closed my eyes and tried to fall back asleep, but I just found myself tossing and turning, the top sheet twisting around my body. Why was I wide awake?

I sat up, my eyes adjusting to the darkness.

Zev was back. He was lying in what looked like the most uncomfortable position, with both feet dangling way off the side of the sofa and one arm over his head. He looked like a cartoon character, a giant in a bed made for one of the Seven Dwarfs. Yet, he still managed to sleep. I was the only one awake.

His glasses were on the end table next to him. He looked so different without them, handsome both ways, but different.

Stop it.

I looked back at the time. I had just spent ten minutes staring at my ex. I needed to do something. I wanted to go back in the bathroom and play the guitar some more, but I didn't want to wake Dylan and Fitz up. On top of everything else, I was not going to be the reason they barely got any rest.

I found my eyes wandering to Zev again. *Enough!*

I grabbed Ruby and my key card and tiptoed into the hall, shutting the door lightly behind me. Zev had excused himself to make his calls earlier. That's what I needed to do—find someplace to play, somewhere with sturdier, better-insulated walls. That's what a responsible human would do.

I knew just the place.

The stairwell. I opened the door and went down until I was between my floor and the one below and sat on one of the steps. I wouldn't sing at full blast or even play Ruby the way I normally would, but I just needed some music, something, anything, to help calm my mind so I could get back to sleep.

I had been avoiding singing "Living, Loving, You," all day, but it really was my best song. I took a deep breath, if I could get through it here, maybe I could end my set with it. It would be the strongest choice.

I took a deep breath and looked at Ruby. "We can do this," I whispered. But I didn't even get to the lyrics, just the guitar intro and I already needed to wipe away tears. It was just too personal. The whole song was how loving him made living that much better. Now, what did that mean? That without him, things would always be a little darker? The song was supposed to be fun, dreamy, whimsical, with a touch of magic. It didn't work if you sobbed your way through it.

I couldn't do it. Instead I went to an old faithful—a Kevin

Wayward song. It wasn't the one I was using for my set, but it was fitting for my mood. It spoke to what I was feeling now. It was about moving on, leaving the past behind, even if it meant leaving a piece of your heart there, too.

I sang it twice, and while it felt cathartic, it didn't make me tired at all. If anything, it energized me. I needed something soothing, something to make me sleepy. The lullaby my dad used to play for my brother and me popped into my head. He wrote the tune and lyrics himself. It wasn't anything fancy or Grammy winning, but to me it was perfect.

Sleep my sweet angel, sleep my love, sleep my baby, dream of the day to come, I sang. As I was about to start the second verse the door to the stairwell slammed shut, and I almost dropped Ruby.

I jumped up. Who was it? Maybe I really should have looked for some mace. I listened to enough news, so I knew what could happen. The stairwell of a hotel in the middle of the night was the equivalent of a dark alley. I didn't even have my stupid heels on me, at least maybe they would have served as a weapon, some sort of dagger.

I turned to face the door, holding Ruby like a bat.

To my relief, it wasn't one of the FBI's Most Wanted, but it *was* someone who made me want to scream. "Zev! You scared me half to death."

"Sorry."

Before I could give him my speech about how I was fed up with his showing up everywhere, he continued talking. "I'm not here to convince you to take me back. I know you need some space. You made that more than clear, and I heard you singing, I heard the . . . ," his voice trailed off. What had he heard? The heartbreak, the pain, the sadness in my voice? I didn't ask. "I just wanted to tell you," he continued, "Trina doesn't have to come tomorrow. The guys told me what you were doing. The train station isn't far from here; I'll just take one back. I didn't want to make you find another way home, I wasn't trying to run you out, I was just trying to understand. I don't know what I did, Sari."

I rolled my eyes at him.

"Okay, I know what I did at the party, but I don't know what happened after. On the plane. One second you were saying we might be okay, and the next you were telling me to get lost."

"I saw your text," I whispered and turned around and sat back down.

I didn't know why I was talking to him. Maybe because he kept doing all these really nice things like offering to take the train home. Or maybe because deep down I wanted to hear his explanation, even if I knew I wouldn't believe it.

"What text?" he asked.

Now he was going to play dumb? "The one from Bethanne. The one that said 'see you tomorrow,' even though you said you had cut off all communication with her. The one that proved you were a liar."

He sat down next to me, and punched something up on his phone. "You mean this text?" he said and handed me the phone. "Scroll back."

I didn't know what he was trying to prove, but curiosity got the better of me. I went to the top. The thread started Thursday night, only it wasn't just to Zev, it was a group text to about a dozen people.

The first text was from Bethanne:

> **BETHANNE**
>
> Hi guys, spring break is almost over. Boo!
> Let's do something. My roof, Saturday night.
> Don't miss it! XOXO

> **MAX**
>
> I'm in.

> **ANDREW**
>
> Me too

Fine, maybe he didn't plan a date with his ex, but he was still having contact with her—getting together in a group more than counted. "You said you told her you wanted nothing to do with her, but *this* is still having something to do with her."

"Keep reading."

I didn't know what he was getting at. I really didn't care that Tali, Zac, Lindy, Megan, and a bunch of other people were all "in" for the get-together, too. Paul's party had a ton of people, and that didn't stop Bethanne and Zev from doing what they did—why would this be any different?

Then I saw it—the text from Zev.

> Please take me off this chain. Not coming,
> you know that.

Oh.

The texts kept coming; she didn't listen. Bethanne and everyone else kept responding. I got to the text that was sent while we were on the plane:

Anger, surprise, relief, sadness, hurt, all rushed through me. I handed the phone back to Zev.

"See it was all a big misunderstanding," he said.

I shook my head. He was talking like this was behind us, like now all could be forgotten, but it couldn't. I was still a wreck from everything that happened. That didn't just go away.

"Zev, it's not that easy."

"Why not? We were fine on the plane—nothing changed. You read a text that I had nothing to do with. This isn't my fault."

He just didn't get it. "You hurt me," I told him, "I don't think you understand that."

"Sari, I've been doing everything to get you back. You're the one who went off on me when I didn't do anything. You don't think that hurt? You wouldn't even hear me out; you just jumped to conclusions. You were willing to throw us out over nothing."

"It wasn't nothing. I saw you kissing another girl. A girl who then posted a picture of the two of you together for the whole school's entertainment."

He took his glasses off and rubbed the bridge of his nose. "And I explained what happened, and you said you got it."

"That was before the text."

He threw up his hands. "The text was nothing. You know that now."

We were going in circles. "But I didn't a minute ago—I thought it was true. If I'm always going to be doubting everything you do, how can we ever work?"

"Because we love each other. You trusted me before. Let's just go back to that."

"I don't know if I can."

He stood up and leaned back against the wall. "This is absurd. Sari, listen to yourself."

"How about *you* listen to me. You have not let up on me all day; you are everywhere. I can't even think straight, Zev. I have the biggest break of my career tomorrow, and all I can focus on is you. I barely practiced. I can't even do my best song because it makes me cry—and I blame you for that."

"That's not my fault."

He kept saying that, and it made me want to blow. "But it feels like it."

His face was turning red. "I don't know what you want me to do, Sari."

Zev was still up against the wall, looking down at me. I felt small, like nothing I said mattered. He just kept pressing. I couldn't think. It was like he needed me to have everything figured out this second and that wasn't possible. It wasn't fair. I turned away from him.

"Sari . . ."

I clutched Ruby to my chest and stared down the steps at the cold, hard concrete below me. If he needed an answer right now, there was only one I could give.

"Maybe you should just go to Bethanne's party," I said.

There was a pause, and his voice hardened. "Maybe I should."

Then he walked up the stairs and out the door, letting it slam behind him.

THIRTY-FIVE

I felt like I was in a daze. Somehow I managed to get Ruby back in her case, but then all I could do was sit there, my face in my hands.

What happened?

There was so much to process, but I just felt numb. The texts, the fight, the storming off, I couldn't even begin to comprehend it all. Was this what I wanted? Did it make a difference? It wasn't up to me anymore, anyway. I told him to go to Bethanne's, and he said okay.

Maybe I should, maybe I should, maybe I should. The words played back in my head in stereo.

I got up, and slowly made my way up the stairs. This was probably for the best. It just hurt so much because the wound was still fresh. It would scab over soon, and eventually it would heal.

I headed back to the room. I'd given Zev enough of a head start.

I put my key card in the slot, but the light wouldn't turn green. "Please," I whispered. I didn't want to knock. I didn't want to deal with Zev again. I didn't want to go all the way back to the lobby. I just wanted to get back under the covers.

I tried the card again.

Still nothing. I collapsed against the door. Why couldn't anything go right?

Gram flashed in my head, and I made myself stand up straight. I needed to stop feeling sorry for myself. "I am capable, confident, and can do whatever I put my mind to," I whispered to myself.

Zev didn't define me.

I was fine before I met him, and I was fine now. I was done with the self-pity. I tried the card three more times, and it finally worked.

I walked inside with my head held high. Dylan and Fitz were still asleep. As for Zev, he was back on the sofa, pretending he was asleep, too. He must have finally reached a point where he didn't want to talk to me any more than I wanted to talk to him. It'd been what I'd been asking for all day . . . all week, even. But now it didn't feel like a win. It didn't feel like anything. I wasn't happy, I wasn't sad, I wasn't angry. I just was done.

THIRTY-SIX

must have dozed off, because the next thing I knew, sun was
streaming into the room and Dylan and Fitz were saying
something to each other on the bed next to me.

I wiped the sleep out of my eyes.

"Did we wake you?" Dylan asked, noticing me stir.

"No, I'm up."

"We were waiting to see if you wanted to go grab breakfast,"
Fitz said. He was already showered and changed. "They have a
buffet."

I looked over at the sofa. Zev was gone; he must have been
down there. "I'll head that way with you, but I'm just going to wait
in the lobby for Trina." I checked the time. I still had awhile before she got here, but I couldn't handle another awkward scene.
And spending the morning pretending to ignore Zev or sitting
at his table like everything was fine both qualified.

Fitz insisted on taking my suitcase down, even though I told
him I could manage.

"Sure you don't want some breakfast?" he asked, once we
were downstairs.

"It's free," Dylan threw in.

"I could bring you something if you're trying to avoid Zev," Fitz offered.

Here he was being Captain America all over again. I guess sometimes first impressions were right. "Thank you. I'm okay, really." And to my own surprise, that was actually the truth. I must have cried myself out. "I'm just going to take one of those apples at the front desk and maybe raid the vending machine, then sit outside and wait for Trina." It stopped raining, and fresh air seemed really nice. I had been cooped up for far too many hours. "Thank you, guys, for everything. Both of you, really. You're amazing."

I went in to give Fitz a hug.

"This isn't good-bye," he said, squeezing me back. "When is your friend getting here?"

"Not sure." She'd texted fifteen minutes ago to say she'd be leaving as soon as humanly possible.

"Well, let us know when she gets here," he said. "And do not leave until we come back down, so we can say a real good-bye."

I nodded. This trip wasn't all bad. I did get to meet Fitz and Dylan, and after what they helped me through, I already counted them as friends.

"Promise?" Dylan said.

"Yeah, I promise."

"And not like one of those promises you gave your mom," he said, and winked at me. "Don't want to have to text Zev to track you down."

"Too soon, man," Fitz said, shaking his head, but he was laughing.

"I thought it could go either way," he answered. His voice was light and playful, and I couldn't help but laugh, too.

I dragged my stuff outside and toward a bench near the entrance to the hotel. The sweet, pungent, distinct smell of a storm was still in the air, but the sky was clear, and I finally felt like I could breathe again.

I sat down and took in the openness around me. No more walls or planes or car doors trapping me. It felt good. I pulled out Ruby and started playing. I was ready for tonight. I felt it.

"That was great," a woman said, when I finished my third song.

I hadn't even realized I had an audience.

"Thanks."

"You should stick with it," she said, before heading to her car. "You've got talent."

Today was already off to a much better start than yesterday.

About forty-five minutes later a familiar car pulled into the lot.

I jumped up.

Finally—Trina was here!

I didn't even put Ruby away, I just raced with her to greet my best friend.

I practically jumped on Trina when she got out of the car.

"Hi," I said, giving her the longest hug in the world. "I am so glad you're here."

"You're going to be happier when you see what I brought you."

She reached into the car and pulled out a pair of flip-flops.

"My savior," I said, and took off my sandals and put them on. Other than the tennis shoes I had thrown out, every pair of shoes that I packed had a heel. While they weren't as bad as the pumps I was stuck in yesterday, my feet were craving flats.

"Should we grab your stuff and get you out of here?" she asked.

"Yes! But I promised the guys I'd say good-bye first."

"Ooh," she said and wiggled her eyebrows. "I get to meet your mystery men."

"Yes, you do."

I texted Fitz:

> Trina is here. About to head out.

> **FITZ**
> Hang on a sec. Be right down.
> We're going to check out now.

We're. That probably meant Zev, too.

My fears were confirmed when they entered the lobby a few minutes later. It was Dylan and Fitz with Zev hanging behind. But that was okay. I was fine. I could handle seeing him. I'd have to do it every day in school until graduation, so I might as well get used to it now.

Trina was not feeling nearly as benevolent. Not only did she totally ignore Zev, but she gave the other two a giant smile. She didn't wait for an introduction. "I'm Trina. You must be Dylan and Fitz," she said, extending her hand. "Just as hot as Sari told me you were."

I shook my head. I knew she was doing this for Zev's benefit.

If I wasn't going to flirt with Fitz and Dylan in front of him, she was going to do it for me. She was as pissed at my ex as I was, maybe more.

"Ignore her," I said. "She speaks the truth, but ignore her." I gave Fitz and Dylan each a hug good-bye. "Thanks again for everything." I was so happy to be leaving, and yet a part of me felt sad. What if this was the last time I saw them? I wanted to hang out again, but I was just a high school senior with boyfriend issues. There was a good chance they'd want nothing more to do with me once we were back in the real world.

"Anytime," Dylan said. "Break a leg tonight. We'd come if it wasn't Gina's party."

"But we'll definitely be at your next one," Fitz added.

"Yeah?" I asked.

"Of course."

"I'd like that." I was going to make an extra effort to keep up the friendship. I had to. Dylan and Fitz were the silver lining to this whole fiasco.

Trina took my backpack and Ruby, and I pulled up the handle of my suitcase and headed toward the car. I looked back at the guys one more time and waved good-bye.

Zev didn't acknowledge me, he hadn't all morning, but I hadn't addressed him, either. We were just two people who no longer had anything to do with each other.

I grabbed my phone and wallet and put the rest of my stuff in Trina's trunk. I got in the car, then texted my mom before she'd have a chance to send Zev another missive.

"Want to grab bagels and coffee for the road?" Trina asked. "I passed a little place on the way here."

"That sounds perfect. You read my mind," I said, putting away my phone.

We drove out of the parking lot and away from Zev.

The bad part of the trip was behind me, I was one step closer to home, and I had my best friend beside me to get me there.

THIRTY-SEVEN

A coffee, bagel with gobs of cream cheese, my best friend—all was right again.

"Okay," Trina said, as she pulled onto the highway. "When you told me Dylan and Fitz were hot. I didn't know you meant *hot* hot. Their GroupIt pictures do not do them justice. Keisha is going to be all over you about a hookup."

"I'll totally do that," I said. "Dylan's taken, but I'll work on Fitz."

"Then she'll owe us one," she said, sounding a little sinister.

"How are things going between you two?" I asked.

"They're actually . . . wait," she said, and bit her lip. "How are *you* doing? You and Zev didn't even look at each other. Do you want to talk about what happened?"

"No." I took a long sip of my coffee. "I am so talked out. I don't even want to think about him anymore. I am sick of me. *Please*, tell me about you. Fill me in on everything."

She looked at me skeptically.

"Seriously, Trina, talk to me. Tell what I missed while I was busy being all poor me and a horrible friend."

"You were not a horrible friend. You had a hard week. This is what we do for each other. We show up. Like you did when my grandfather died."

Trina had been a wreck. She and her grandpa had been incredibly close.

"And *you* when Quinn did that whole Jabba the Hutt thing," I said.

"*You* when I panicked and almost didn't go in to take my SATs. We could do this all day. But the point is, you don't need to thank me *or* apologize. This is us."

She was right. "So are you going to tell me what's been going on or what?" I asked, trying to lighten the mood. I wanted to hear fun stories and laugh and put yesterday behind me.

Trina told me more about the books she read over break (she got five in—two rom-coms, a fantasy, a sci-fi, and one nonfiction about mechanical engineering). She gave me her mini reviews. They all sounded like things I'd be interested in except the last one, which was totally out of my league. The rest she sold me on. Some people went to Goodreads for recommendations, I didn't need to. I had Trina.

She filled me in on what she and Mike were up to. They saw the latest superhero blockbuster. She had a family day, they went to her aunt and uncle's to celebrate her little cousin's birthday. And then there was the NYU party with her sister. "It's weird," she said, "I never really thought of Keisha as a friend, just a know-it-all big sister, but she's actually been nice—and fun. Don't get me wrong, she's still acting all *you need to listen to me*, but it's different."

"That's amazing." I always liked Keisha. I wouldn't mind

hanging out with her more, especially if I could make her and Fitz happen.

"And you know that dress of hers? The one I salivate over that she never lets me touch?"

"The one that's like a Greek goddess dress?"

"Yes," she said, practically jumping in her seat. "Guess who gets to wear it to prom?"

"No way! Trina, you are going to look stunning. You have to try it on for me."

"We'll have a little fashion show and figure out how we're going to wear our hair and do our makeup," she said.

"Sounds good." Only, I had no idea what I was going to do about prom now. I wasn't sure I even wanted to go anymore. Trina, Trevor, and the rest of our group would never let me stay home, but it wasn't going to be the way I had envisioned it. I did already have a dress, though. Floor length, emerald green, with a cinched waist and a cut-out above the chest. I saw it before homecoming, but it was too expensive, so I started stalking it online, waiting for it to go on sale. When it did, I snatched it up.

"Oh my God," Trina said, lightly hitting the steering wheel. "I can't believe I brought up prom today."

"It's fine. Really." It was just one of those things I was going to have to get used to. It was probably for the best that I get accustomed to it now.

This time she was the one to change the subject. "What are you wearing tonight?" she asked. "It's your big performance. You need something killer."

"I was going to wear this," I said, and gestured to my current dress. "But since I'll have lived in it for more than twenty-four hours, I think something else is in order."

"Good call," she said. "What about a pair of nice jeans and that red top, the super cleavagey one?"

It was one of my favorites, but it sometimes fell a little too low and needed readjusting, I didn't want to have to deal with a wardrobe malfunction during my first real gig. "Not for this one. Maybe my black-and-white tank?"

She scrunched her nose. "Seems a little casual."

I really had no idea what to wear.

"I got it," Trina said. "Your talent show dress. You haven't worn it in ages, and it looks beautiful on you."

It was a blue wrap dress that was the same shade as my eyes. I hadn't tried it on in a while, but I was pretty sure it would still fit. "I think that might be the one," I said.

I was getting excited. This was really happening. I was performing at Meta! We went over my hair—down and wavy. My jewelry—minimal. Just a pair of gold hoops. Shoes—ballet flats. Definitely no heels.

"I think you're all set," she said.

"Just have to calm my nerves." It wasn't stage fright, just jitters over my first real legit gig.

"I know what to do for that."

Trina punched up a cringe-worthy love-to-hate pop song on her stereo and blasted the volume. She didn't have to tell me what to do. We both started singing as loud as we could, letting our voices fill the car while we danced in our seats.

"Look out the window," Trina said a little while later, breaking up our car concert.

We were exiting the FDR Drive onto Second Avenue. We were in the city! I was back. I felt a sense of relief as we drove by the familiar buildings, restaurants, and bodegas. Manhattan never looked so good.

Trina pulled up in front of my building, and I was smiling so wide, my cheeks hurt, but I couldn't stop.

After everything I'd been through, I was finally home!

THIRTY-EIGHT

Despite a heavy suitcase, a guitar, and a backpack, I practically floated to my apartment. It felt so good to be back. Trina told me to call her if I needed anything, but I was fine now. I made it home with time to spare. I thanked her but let her know I'd see her tonight.

I didn't even get my key all the way in when my mother opened the door and threw her arms around me. All the anger and annoyance I felt the other day melted away as I squeezed her back. It felt safe in her arms, familiar.

"There she is," my dad said, joining us. "Do I get a turn?"

I hugged him, too, and after I pulled away they both just stood there, staring at me. They looked so relieved to see me, that it almost made me want to cry. Happy tears this time.

"It's only been a week," I said, finally dropping my stuff. "You're acting like I've been gone a year."

"We were worried," my mom said.

"I know. Thank you, but now you can see for yourself, I'm fine." I was more than fine.

"We're happy you're home," my dad said. "It was too quiet here without you."

"You mean nice," my brother yelled from the living room.

I headed toward him. "Don't you mean boring?" I dropped next to him on the couch and pulled him toward me. "You know you missed your big sister," I told him, cradling him like he was my baby.

He tried to push me away, but I wouldn't let go.

"Did not," he said, but he was smiling.

"Yes, you did," I said, in singsong voice. "And lucky for you, I'm going to college nearby just so I can come back and bug you all the time."

"I hear there are some good schools in Alaska," he said, pulling away and trying to give me a noogie.

Back to normal had never felt so good.

My set was at eight, and I wanted to get there no later than seven. That still gave me time to take a nap and get ready.

I took off the dress and threw it in the hamper. It felt good to get out of that thing. I took a quick shower and then crawled into my bed. *My* bed. Oh, how I missed it. It was the perfect balance of firm and soft. Goldilocks would never have left, and at the moment, I didn't want to, either. I set my alarm, snuggled up against my blanket and closed my eyes.

A persistent beep filled my room. Had it been three hours already?

Normally, I would have hit snooze, but tonight was too big a deal to risk oversleeping. I wasn't messing around. I got out of bed, searched my closet for the blue dress, and started getting ready.

As I was putting on the final touches of my makeup at my desk, there was a knock on my door.

"Sari, can I come in?" my mom asked.

"Yeah," I said, closing my mascara tube and studying my work in the little stand mirror.

Mom nodded her head at me in approval. "Wow, I have one beautiful daughter."

"Thanks."

She sat down on the edge of my bed and patted the spot next to her. She wanted me to come sit. I hoped this wasn't about my lack of communication or her texting Zev. I really didn't want to get into that now.

I moved beside her and waited.

"How are you doing?"

I was getting kind of tired of people asking me that, but I answered, "Great."

"No, really," she said. "I'm still worried about you."

"Well, don't. I'm safe. I'm out of the storm. You're seeing me with your own eyes. Everything's good."

"I meant because of what's happening with you and Zev."

I sucked in some air. She was doing this *now*? "Nothing's happening with us. We're over. I told you that." And I had been trying very hard not to dwell on it. Why was she bringing it up? "I'm past it."

"You're past it?"

Was she going to repeat all my words back to me? "Yep." I cried myself out yesterday and all last week. Today was a new day. I was moving forward.

"All right." She didn't say anything else, she just put her arm around me and pulled me to her shoulder. And I don't know why, but my eyes started to well up again and my body started to shake. It was like my mom was seeing through me, and I couldn't keep up the facade anymore. There was something about being there with her that made me just want to unload it all.

"Let it out," she said.

And I did. I told her everything. The kiss. The explanation. The text. The stress. The fight.

"Well, it sounds to me," she said, "the question here isn't about love. It's clear that's still there. It's about trust."

"How am I ever supposed to do that again?" I wiped my eyes and black mascara came off on the back of my hand. Crap. Now on top of everything else, I was going to have to redo my makeup. "Seeing Zev and Bethanne together . . ." I took a deep breath and let it out. "I never want to feel that way again."

"I know." She ran her fingers through my hair. "But, sweetie, part of love is opening your heart. You have to take a risk sometimes."

"I did and look where it got me."

"It's upsetting, and sometimes you'll get hurt. Relationships take work. They need trust. Despite what all those songs you live on say, love by itself isn't enough. And if you can't trust Zev, then you're right to end it."

I grabbed a tissue from my end table and blew my nose.

"*But,*" she continued, "if this isn't about him, and it's about fear—fear of getting hurt, fear of the unknown, fear of what you can't control, fear of whatever, you're going to miss out. Yes, sometimes there will be pain, sometimes people will disappoint you, sometimes even intentionally, but that doesn't mean you should ever close off your heart." She pulled me closer to her. "Love is a gift. All kinds of love. Family. Friends. A partner. To give it, to receive it, it's so much more powerful than fear."

"But how do I know something like before won't happen again?"

"You don't. That's why you have to decide if you trust him or not—if you believe his explanation."

I did. At least I think I did. "And then what?"

"Then you take it from there. If you don't trust him, then you're done. If you do, then you can't question his every move. If you worry over every text, every time he doesn't pick up the phone, you'll drive yourself and those around you up a wall."

That was true. When my mom was checking up on me every three seconds yesterday, I wanted to scream. Still, I was starting to understand. The not knowing was scary.

"Sari, there are no guarantees in life. We all just do the best that we can. I wish I could take away your pain. I wish I could tell you no one will ever break your heart again, but I can't. But I *can* tell you, you won't regret loving someone. There's no better feeling. Whether it's with Zev or someone new, don't close yourself off from loving—that's not a way to live."

"What do I do about him?" I was still so confused.

"I can't tell you that, either. That's up to you. But if you listen to your head, your heart, your gut, they'll guide you. Whatever you decide, you'll get through this, and I will be here for you every step of the way."

While that didn't give me the answer, somehow knowing she'd be there helped.

THIRTY-NINE

My dad let out a low whistle when I came out of my room. "Are you sure we can't come?"

"Next time, I promise," I said. This wasn't their crowd, and I didn't want to worry about what they were thinking or if they'd try to chat up Sheila. I could picture my dad laying it on thick, and while totally sweet, Sheila was not exactly the sentimental type.

"Knock 'em dead," he said.

My mom snapped a picture on her phone, and even Dan congratulated me.

This was real. I was on my way to Meta.

I got there super early. Other than for a couple of employees, the place was empty. I took the time to sound check and warm up. Even then I still had more than an hour to kill.

They told me I could wait backstage. *Backstage!*

I thought I might hyperventilate. I'd never been allowed in this area before. I felt such a burst of energy as I opened the door and went down a narrow hall to my dressing room.

I had a *dressing room*! I wanted to shout it to the world.

It didn't matter that it wasn't the fanciest or that it also doubled as a storage room; it was mine, and this was epic.

I was standing in the same place that *Kevin Wayward*, Grammy winners, and some of the biggest names in music stood. I was on my way. I sat in the chair and let my thoughts roam. They started with how I had dreamed of being here for so long, but pretty soon that brought me to Zev. I had always pictured him here with me. Everything my mom said rolled around in my brain. Zev *said* Bethanne kissed him. I believed him before I saw that group text. Why was it so hard for me to get back to that place?

I needed to stop. I could drown myself in these thoughts. Right now, I had a show to get ready for. It was getting closer.

I tried to meditate, but I was too amped up. I was the first set of the night. I'd be going on soon.

"Fifteen minutes," Craig, one of the employees, came back to tell me.

"Thanks."

I decided to peek out at the crowd. I spotted Trina and waved. She was at a table with Mike, Trevor, and Dom. No sign of Zev, but I guess I should have expected that. I told him not to come. Had he taken my words to heart? Had he gone to Bethanne's?

I *really* had to stop this train of thought.

I looked around the rest of the room. It definitely wasn't a Kevin Wayward–sized crowd, but there were people. They didn't need to remove any tables and chairs, but a good number of seats were taken. That was kind of impressive.

The place normally picked up later on Saturdays. My set was

fairly early. But I didn't care. I was at Meta, and an actual audience was going to watch me perform. An audience that was alive with possibilities.

I returned backstage and the ten-minute call came.

Then the five.

I found myself bouncing up and down and quietly running through the scales.

Then one minute.

I picked up Ruby. This was it.

Craig was onstage introducing me. "Welcome to Meta," he said. "Our first performer tonight is making her debut here. She's just eighteen years old but has an incredibly powerful voice. Let's give it up for Sari Silver."

I walked out and waved as the crowd applauded. I heard Trina scream my name. I felt a nervous energy. Not exactly scared but more excited or rather electrified. This was finally happening. I was onstage at the greatest club in the world. I pulled the stool in front of the microphone and took a seat with Ruby on my lap.

"Hi, everyone. It's so amazing to be here, and I have some great songs for you." I introduced my first one, a Kevin Wayward ballad and began to play. For most of it, I was pretty aware of my surroundings of what was happening, of how important this night was. But by the time I made it to the second one, "The Wonder of It," I loosened up. I was able to get lost in my playing, into that music high that I loved. It was pretty exhilarating. Before I knew it, it was time for my last song.

I began to play.

Only I wasn't playing the song I had been planning to do. I was playing the one I had written for Zev—"Living, Loving, You."

Lost in the music, in the moment, my heart knew what it wanted. It knew what *I* wanted. Being up there in front of the crowd, it was like a fog had lifted, and the decision was made. Just like that, I knew the song was what I had to play.

Living you is loving.

Loving you is living.

Living, loving, you.

Living, loving, you.

My mom's words had come back to me. *Don't close yourself off from loving—that's not a way to live.*

She was basically paraphrasing my song lyrics, I just hadn't seen it. Zev made living so much better.

I was not going to lose that. Not over fear. I didn't let nerves keep me from doing my music, and I wasn't going to let it keep me from the guy who made me laugh, and feel beautiful and loved—even if we did hit a rocky patch.

I knew what I had to *do.*

I had to get Zev back.

I finished the song, and the crowd erupted. Well, Trina and her table erupted, the rest of the audience gave a really nice round of applause. I took a bow and looked out at the crowd.

I never felt a rush like that in my life. I was doing what I loved, what I dreamed of. My friends were there to support me, and even people I never met were applauding. There was just one thing missing, one person I needed to make this night complete.

It was time to take a chance.

What Zev and I had was worth fighting for, and that's exactly what I was going to do.

FORTY

I went backstage, grabbed my phone and texted Zev.

> I want to talk. Please. I'm sorry.

I could see that he read it, but no reply came. Not even those little dots that showed someone was typing.

I tried again.

> Where are you? Can I come meet you?

I waited. He was ignoring me. Maybe I deserved that, but I wasn't going to give up.

> I love you.

"I love you, too."

I swung around. It was Zev.

"You're here," I said.

He was leaning against the door frame. "I wasn't going to miss this."

I took a step toward him. "I looked out in the audience, but I didn't see you there."

"I came in right at the start and stayed in the corner. I didn't want to throw you off. I didn't know if you wanted me here."

"I did." I moved closer to him, until I was leaning on the other side of the door frame.

We stood there, just looking at each other. He was waiting for me to speak, but I didn't even know where to start.

"Zev . . . I . . ."

I shook my head, letting my hair spill over my face. Seeing him, I felt excited and awkward and shy and totally at a loss for words.

He reached out, moving my hair back behind my ear. His hand touched my cheek, and I shivered.

Then I just let the words spill. "Zev, I should have heard you out. I should have let you explain. I was just so hurt and confused. I needed time to think."

"And I should have given it to you."

"I don't want us to be over," I said.

"Neither do I." He smiled, and I reached up and touched his dimple.

"You played my song," he said and moved closer to me.

"It felt right." I inched in, too, until just a hair separated us. Our bodies weren't touching, but I could feel a current between us, like that electrically charged force that keeps two magnets apart until the pull is too strong to resist.

"You know what else is right?" he asked.

"What?"

"This." Zev stepped in again, until there was no space

between us. He put his hands through my hair, lifting my face toward his.

My heartbeat quickened and my lips parted slightly. Zev leaned down and kissed me. Slow and gentle at first, and then more greedily, neither of us wanting to pull away.

It felt new and old again, and I didn't want it to stop. As his arms wrapped around me, and his lips continued to press into mine, I knew we were the stuff of love songs.

This was what home felt like.

ACKNOWLEDGMENTS

In some ways, this is the hardest part to write, because I can't come close to expressing how thankful I am for all the help, guidance, and support I've received while working on this book.

Jonathan Yaged and Jean Feiwel: Being a part of Swoon Reads and Macmillan is a dream come true. Thank you for this amazing opportunity.

Holly West and Lauren Scobell: Where do I start? You both leave me in awe with all that you do. Please know how appreciative I am for your notes, edits, advice, and friendship.

The more people I meet at Swoon and Macmillan, the more I realize just how lucky I am. From the subrights, sales, marketing, publicity, digital, and advertising teams to the production and copy editors, the designers, assistants, interns, and everyone else I've had the pleasure of working with on this journey—you all make this experience a truly wonderful one. Thank you so much.

Laura Dail: Your kindness, expertise, and advice continue to amaze me—and keep me on course—as I navigate the writing world. Thank you for all that you (and your team) do. It is very appreciated.

To all the librarians, booksellers, bloggers, reviewers, readers, and the Swoon community, thank you for spending time with Sari and her friends.

To my colleagues and friends at Fox 5, you guys are awesome! Your support of my books (and me) means a lot. And a special shout-out to Audrey Puente who helped me figure out a weather nightmare scenario for a time of year that tends to be pretty calm in the Northeast, and to Lou Albanese, who, for *My New Crush Gave to Me*, helped me figure out some football plays.

My latest books have all shown close, supportive friendships. I didn't have to go far for inspiration. I truly am blessed with incredible friends. You all mean so much to me.

The same goes for my family. I don't know what I'd do without you.

Mom, Jordan, Andrea, Liam, and Alice—my heart is filled with so much love for you all. Always know you mean the world to me.

I wish my dad were here, so I could share this all with him. Knowing what he'd say doesn't make up for the loss, but it does remind me of how much he loved his family—and we him.

And finally, to the airline that left me stranded for hours (and ultimately detoured me to Michigan)—I came up with this book during that delay. You showed me how to make the most of a bad situation. So for that, thank you, but next time, I'd really prefer to take off on time. ☺

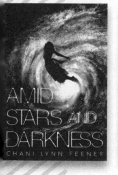

DID YOU KNOW...

readers like you helped to get this book published?

Join our book-obsessed community and help us discover awesome new writing talent.

1 **Write it.**
Share your original YA manuscript.

2 **Read it.**
Discover bright new bookish talent.

3 **Share it.**
Discuss, rate, and share your faves.

4 **Love it.**
Help us publish the books you love.

Share your own manuscript or dive between the pages at **swoonreads.com** or by downloading the **Swoon Reads app.**